Sheep Among Wolves

Published by Spines
ISBN: 979-8-89383-129-0

Sheep Among Wolves

Rat In A Cage

CD Franklin

Contents

Chapter 1

"They teach us about the "dark ages" in school. Its drilled into our heads, and yet there's still some that don't fully believe it was real. After all, it does sound ridiculous. Humans were the dominant species and the wolves were the slaves? Sounds too good to be true. But, they say things were very different back then. It was over a thousand years ago after all.

The wolves, or werewolves as the humans called them, couldn't shift any time they wanted back then, but instead they only shifted on the full moon, in a violent display of cracking bones and pain so intense they would usually pass out. And when they were in wolf form, their minds were more beast than man so they had less conscious control over their thoughts, making them easier to track. The humans feared them and so they hunted them down, taking advantage of the shift when they were at their weakest and most vulnerable. Women and children were often slaughtered as to reduce their population, but the men were typically captured and forced into slavery. Even in human form they were stronger than most men so they were great for manual labor. Shackled and collared with silver, their only true weakness. Externally, silver simply prevents them from shifting, but if they get cut with it, it can be toxic, depending on how bad the wound is. Which is why it was all mined out and destroyed centuries ago. But back in those days, it was in abundance and the humans used it at any chance they got. Some even made cages for the wolves out of silver lined bars. They'd remove their shackles and collars on the full moon and force them to fight to the death for their own sick entertainment. Honestly, I do understand why they hated the humans so much.

But then came the great uprising. A story every man, woman, and child knows by heart because it's told to us every year from the time we're in kindergarten all the way up until we graduate. How Marrok the Great liberated the wolves and became the first true alpha.

Back then the wolves were scattered, hiding for their own protection out in the woods. Marrok lived out there with his small family, deeply shrouded in thick trees. They lived a peaceful life, rarely needing to worry about the humans. One summer morning, he awoke a short distance from his home after he had passed out the night before from a shift. He heard his family's screams and ran back to his small cabin to see human men slitting the throats of his eldest daughter, his wife's lifeless body already turning grey in a pool of blood. His youngest daughter, clothes ripped from her body was being held with arms out stretched, pulled by the wrists by men on either side of her. One of the men drew his sword and drove it into her stomach, running her threw. He pulled the blade from her as blood poured quickly from the wound. Her little face quickly lost all color.

Marrok let out a great cry that alerted the men of his presence. When they saw him, they threw the lifeless bodies aside and came after him. He flew into a rage unlike anything that anyone had seen before and fought the men. There were half a dozen of them so he was largely outnumbered, but as they all crowded in on him, his anger caused him to begin to shift. Something that was, up until that point, impossible during daylight hours. What's more, it was so fast that the bone cracking pain happened all in one burst, meaning he didn't pass out and was only a little woozy for a moment.

When the men saw him, towering over them, covered in fur, the face of a wolf, standing like a man, snarling, fists clenched, ready for a fight, they knew they were dead, so they ran as quickly as they could, to little avail.

He grabbed one and tore him to shreds in seconds. The next was slashed across the back, cracking his spine. Marrok grabbed another by the throat, lifting the man in the air. He tightened his grip forcefully, crushing the man's vertebrae, killing him nearly instantly. One man ran, the very one that had killed his youngest daughter. Marrok leapt onto his back, sending him crashing to the ground. He sunk his teeth into the man's neck and tore a massive chunk out of his throat and shoulder, causing blood to spray all over the ground.

Two of the men managed to escape in the chaos, but with all the others already dead, Marrok fell to his knees and howled a long, lonely howl that turned into sobs as he gently shifted back to human form. Laying his family to rest in the morning sunlight, he decided to make it his mission to not only take revenge on the humans but to over throw them so that no other wolves would have to die this way.

He searched for weeks to find other wolves. They were reluctant at first to join his cause, fearing that it was hopeless and impossible. They were so greatly outnumbered and couldn't fight against the humans silver weapons. But once he showed them how he had been training his body to shift at will, they came to his side, naming him their great alpha.

On the next full moon, they tracked down the two men that had escaped and laid waste to their town. Marrok had greater control over his thoughts while in the shift now and was able to lead the others to decimate the whole town, but made sure that those two men were left alive. As dawn approached, there were mostly only women and children left alive in the small village. The wolves had killed almost all of the men. The sunlight began to crest over the horizon, illuminating the gory scene of blood trickling down the cobblestone streets, sprayed on every brick home and flowing down gutters like a red river. The wolves gritted their teeth and braced against the pain. Some shifted back to human form, though in a less dramatic fashion than before. Some struggled against the change and were able to retain wolf form, though somewhat weakened. They pulled any and all remaining survivors out to stand in the town square. The two men that Marrok kept alive, the two that killed his wife and daughters, were bruised from attacks from the wolves, but otherwise unharmed. Marrok, still in wolf form, grabbed them by the backs of the shirts and dragged them to the fountain in the center of the small town square, pushing his way through the frightened townsfolk. He stood up on the fountain base and lifted the men up by the collars of their shirts. In a deep, and powerful voice, never heard before from a wolf, he spoke. "Let these men, no, these filthy vermin stand as a symbol of our growing strength and the many changes to come. We are superior and we shall rise! Forced into the shadows no more, we will rule and all humans will obey lest you become one of these bodies, lifeless and rotting. For all that oppose us shall meet the same fate." He then threw one of the men to the ground where a wolf instantly grabbed him tightly as the man struggled, fruitlessly to get away. Marrok ushered some wolves over to hold the arms of the man still with his grips, outstretched. He grabbed a sword off the ground, seeing again in his mind the man drive the sword through his daughters stomach. And with that image, as a tear rolled down from his golden eye, he ran the man through. The man let out a small gasp as blood slowly poured from the wound. Marrok watched the light slowly fade from his eyes, but just before it was extinguished completely, he pulled the sword out and nodded to a wolf that quickly came up behind him and drove his fangs into the man's shoulder and tore out a chunk of meat from his shoulder and neck, killing him. Marrok took the other man and killed him in the exact same manner. The remaining townspeople watched with shock and horror. And that was the day that the world changed.

Such a fun story for kindergartners.

Now that at least some of the wolves could change at will, they were able to take over the town. They taught others how to control the shift, but as time went on, the wolves themselves began to change. No one is exactly sure why, but from that day on, they began to evolve. Wolves started being born able to shift at will, their minds were much more stable and controlled while in wolf form, and the shift was fast and increasingly pain free. Before long, shifting was effortless. While in wolf form, they were less like wild beasts and now more like beautiful, powerful creatures that were the perfect combination of man and wolf. Their minds grew sharper, their instincts more refined and strength and senses even more acute. The only thing that remained the same was their allergy to silver. Some humans say it was the only gift the great creator gave us. A weakness that could, just maybe help us take back our world some day.

Me personally, I don't know if I believe that. After all, humans haven't gotten their hands on silver in nearly 3 centuries. But most don't give it much thought and some even say we should be grateful for those days. The wolves became much more intelligent than humans and transformed our world from one of squalor and dirt, to glittering, technologically advanced cities all over the world. Now they hardly ever shift into wolf form because they simply don't need to.

They developed technology to predict a humans behavior and personality and began separating the humans into 4 distinct classes, starting at the age of 18. One thing about the wolves, they never harm a child.

Chapter 2

Shortly after someone's 18th birthday, the wolves come to them with the scanner. A small device placed on someone's head that reads brain wave patterns or something like that and tells them things about their personality and their probability of them fighting against the system. I don't really understand how it all works, but then no human really does, that's just one of the many secrets they keep. The human will place their left hand in a small device that uses a laser to print a symbol signifying their class on the back of their hand. It's not just a symbol like some ordinary tattoo. It holds all of their information like a digital fingerprint. It's a form of identification that is used for anything and everything. Anywhere identification is required, whether its paying at the store, going to the doctor, getting on a bus, anything at all, they have to put the back of their hand to a scanner that reads their mark. Every mark is a black circle with different symbols in each one for the different classes.

There are the Devout, who's symbol is a golden capital D with a purple paw print inside of it. They are those who sympathize with the wolves, even love them, or at the very least suck up to them. Some do it because the Devout get all the money and power. They are placed in the wealthiest districts with the best houses and jobs. Most grow up to be lawyers or politicians or work for the wolves in some way. Of course, our judicial system is a joke, in my opinion so I don't even really know why we have lawyers.

There's very little crime, that's true, but at a high cost. All prisoners are sent to jail, but no one stays there long. Once a year we have Judgment Day on the anniversary of the Great Uprising. It's a global holiday and everyone gets off work. Every town has a huge arena that can fit pretty much everyone in the whole town, some towns even have more than one. Everyone is forced to go, though most treat it like a sporting event or celebration and wouldn't need to be forced at all. At the center of the arena stands a large podium where the Judge, the most powerful man in town, sits and looks down on a smaller podium where the accused stands. They're chained like animals in a cage at the back and brought to the stand. A lawyer explains to the judge what they are accused of and presents evidence. There is rarely ever a defense as there are cameras all over the place in the city limits that record everything. Their punishment depends on their crime and comes in degrees of severity. For minor crimes like theft, robbery, or things like that, they are taken to the left side of the arena and stepped up to an operating table. They are given pain medication and a Tracker is inserted in their eye. It's a nearly invisible device that shows not only video of everything the person sees and hears, but also gives data on their mental state and vitals and can predict if they are planning to repeat their crime. This acts as the ultimate probation and the conditions and length of their probation can vary some depending on the crime. Once their probation is up, they go to the doctor to have it removed. When they place it, they put a tiny brand near the eye that shows everyone that they were a criminal.

If they commit murder, they are taken to the right side of the arena, where they stand on a stone slab, their shackles hooked up to the chains in shining steel columns that keep their arms outstretched, and executed. There are three degrees of execution, First degree entails placing a ring on their head. After a short countdown the device sends an electrical charge to their brain, frying it instantly. This is usually what happens to those who kill humans. Quick and painless, this is by far the best option. Second degree is for those that kill wolves or kill multiple people. They get their throats sliced from behind. They feel the fear, the pain, and they bleed out in a couple of minutes. Its horrible.

Third degree is reserved for the worst of the worst. Those that kill the highest members of wolf society. No one has been given a third degree execution in decades. At this point, no one is dumb enough to commit such a murder. We're told that a third degree execution is where the person is run through with a sword, then bitten and torn to shreds, just like those men during the great uprising, though few have lived long enough to have seen it first hand. Many cheer on the executions, seeing it as exciting and the eradication of dangerous criminals, but there are many that hate seeing it, and yet they can't look away. The whole thing is recorded and not only broadcasted on T.V for any that couldn't make it in person, but also put up on a huge screen in the arena so that no matter where you are in the stadium, you can see everything up close. If you can't make it in person, you have to apply for a pass in order to stay home. If it's denied, you are required to go to the stadium like everyone else, but if it is granted, the broadcast will automatically come on any device you have at home, and you can't turn it off. They want it made abundantly clear that crime of any sort will not be tolerated, but more importantly, that they hold the ultimate control.

The Devout are not only ingrained in this system, they love the system and do everything they can to support it. Most love the wolves simply out of jealousy and a desire to have as much control and power as possible. If they can't be the highest in the food chain, they will settle for the second highest, even if it means turning against their own species. I guess I can't entirely blame them, but it's still slimy and disgusting. Some are actually dumb enough to think that the wolves will somehow turn them into a wolf, though everyone knows that's impossible. Wolves are born, not made. But some still cling to the delusional hope. Under the Devout are the Guard.

The Guard are police, first responders, doctors, etc. Their symbol is a blue and silver shield with a red capital G in front of it. They don't necessarily love the system but uphold their laws because they know that if they don't, many more lives would be lost. They are typically good people that want to keep everyone safe, even if it means enforcing laws they don't agree with. They live in districts near the center of town, usually near important areas such as the judges house, schools, banks, the stadiums, etc. Because of this they live in pretty nice houses, though not as nice as the Devout.

The largest class is the Neutral class. Their symbol is a black hand print with a white N in front of it. These are just average people. Those that don't particularly love or hate the wolves and go along with their rules because it's all they know. They don't want to make waves and just want to live a normal life. They have all the regular jobs like store clerk, construction, teacher, etc. Neutrals live in the outer ring of the city in modest but cozy houses, depending somewhat on the job they have. The vast majority of humans are in the Neutral class, but there is one more. The Vermin.

These are those who harbor a deep hatred for the wolves and their laws and will likely fight against the system at some point in their lives. These people are exiled from society and forced to live in squalor either far out of the city or down in the sewers. If any are caught above ground in the city limits, they are taken to prison and sometimes executed for whatever crime they want to make up. Everyone dreads getting labeled as Vermin or having a child labeled as Vermin.

The symbol for the Vermin is a large, lime green V and above it is a repulsive looking rat head with scars and green eyes. When someone gets marked as a Vermin, they are taken against their will to be medically sterilized and thrown out of town. Many choose to stay out in the woods, but some don't. While its easier to not get caught out there, it can be harder to find food for those who aren't experienced at catching animals or foraging. Anyone who finds a Vermin anywhere near the city is, shall we say, strongly encouraged to report it and often the Vermin are hunted down and killed. So many stay below the city in the maze of sewers and tunnels for all the electrical wires, and pipes that service the city. Everyone knows they are down there, and as long as they stay down there, they are largely over looked. I can't imagine what it must be like down there, but I try not to think about it much.

CHAPTER 3

Now that you know about our world, I can introduce myself. My name is Christina Redding. I'm writing this in the hopes that someday our world may be different and people can use this as insight into how we lived. Everyone thinks it's a regular journal, and in a lot of ways it is, but it's also more than that.

My father is in the Guard and a loyal police officer. He and I have always been inseparable. My mom and I on the other hand, have always had a tense relationship. She was marked as a Neutral and maybe she used to be, but as time has gone on, she has started to understand the wolves more and almost seems like a Devout at times.

I'm an only child, but that's not unusual. Most families only have one or 2 children because the more children they have, the more risk of one of them being marked as a Vermin and being taken away.

I live next door to my best friend Aliyah Larson, or as everyone calls her, Allie. Her dad Robert is a Guard and my dad's partner and best friend. He's more like an Uncle to me and I even call him Uncle Robert, even though he and my dad look absolutely nothing alike. He is dark skinned, tall but with a stocky, slightly muscular build. His wife, who passed away a few years back of cancer, had a fair complexion with the most beautiful, shiny black hair, a trait that Allie inherited, along with her beautiful almond, almost cat shaped eyes, which is why she got the nickname "Allie Cat". Allie is so beautiful with caramel skin, dark brown eyes, long, shiny black hair, and a smile that could melt icebergs. She seriously looks like a model and has a bright and cheerful personality that makes everyone love her. She's a mix of cool rock and roll, and cheerful girly style, with a hint of athleticism. She's tall and lean with just the right amount of curves. I've always, not so secretly, been jealous of her. I'm shorter, have brown hair with a slight wave to it and way too much frizz that I can never seem to get to grow much longer than my shoulders. My skin is pretty light with a pinkish undertone and I burn easily in the sun. Freckles cover my nose and I have a short, pointed chin and a squatty, squared off face. The only thing I kind of like about my face is my soft green eyes. They're the exact same color as my dad's. Everyone says I look a lot like him. I have very little curves and feel like I look like a 10 year old boy. But I suppose that's what I get for being in track most of my life.

Allie and I are the same age and our birthdays are just 3 weeks apart. My birthday is November 4th, hers is the 27th. Her little brother Jake is 13 and they're pretty close, though he is getting to the age where he's pushing her away more. Allie and I are super close and have a ton in common. We both love the same movies, have similar styles, though she's more into pink and I like dark green, and she has a better fashion sense. I usually just wear jeans and a hoodie or tee shirt where she wears more form fitting clothes and matching jewelry with simple but bright makeup. We're both obsessed with the same band, Black Knight Rebellion and it's lead singer Caleb Knight, a.k.a, the hottest guy alive. We have most classes together, except for a few and go to lunch together every day. We have quite a few friends, mostly girls on the track team, but I don't know if I'd classify us as popular or not. Allie maybe, but it feels like I'm more just tagging along most of the time. Our dreaded rival is Blair Jackson. The most popular girl in school and a total bitch. Her ice blue eyes are always covered in purple eyeshadow, thick black eyeliner and fluffy fake lashes. Her shiny dark brown hair falls down in perfect waves, nothing like the chaotic, random waves that I have. Everyone knows that she'll be marked as Devout and she brags about it all the time. Both of her parents are Devout and rich beyond belief. In the ultimate cliché, she's the head cheerleader and dating the quarterback Matt Harrison. He's hot, but dense. And he might as well be her little pet. He wears matching purple outfits and does anything and everything she asks. They both put Devout symbols on everything and wear them like name brands they flash to show off their wealth and power. Matt's flunky is Cory James and the 3 of them are always together

The new school year is starting soon and I can't help but have mixed feelings about it. I'm excited to finally be a senior, but it also means that we'll be turning 18 in a few months. And unlike Allie, who seems convinced she's going to be marked as Neutral, I worry that I'll be put in the Guard like my dad. And that isn't exactly thrilling.

I grew up seeing my dad come home from long days, tired and stressed. He always did his best to put on a happy face for me, but I would over hear him and my mom talking about how he hated putting away young kids that stole something from a convenience store, knowing that they'd get branded as a criminal for the rest of their life, or how he couldn't stand having to bring in Vermin, knowing that their only real crime was hating the wolves, and how wrong it was that that alone was a crime punishable by death. He didn't like the law but he knew that if he didn't enforce it, the wolves would kill innocent people just to prove that they are in control. It's happened before a few times throughout history and every time it has ended in a blood bath. While our judicial system seems barbaric, it does serve its purpose. There's very little serious crime and hardly any wars to speak of throughout history since the Great Uprising. For the most part, people live in peace. There are few that are very poor, most do fairly well, and most everyone lives normal lives. The wolves, for all their faults, have made our world pretty comfortable for us, something they really didn't have to do. Especially given our history. They do rule over us with a tight grip and while our lives are peaceful, we aren't free. But if we keep our heads down and stick to the rules, things can be pretty good. And the Guard ensure that. He believed that with every fiber of his being at first, but lately his faith has been wavering And with my mom's views changing in the other direction, it's lead to many fights between them and I keep feeling like they're gonna tell me any day now that they're getting a divorce.

Judgment day is in a week. The whole town is buzzing about it. And I'm getting my yearly knot in my stomach. Most everyone loves it. They get a day off of work, there's cheering, food vendors, its grotesque in my personal opinion. I understand it, but do they have to turn it into some sort of celebration? Even though it's a month and a half before school starts, most of the older kids are usually still talking about it on the first day of school, especially if anything "exciting" happens. I'm just trying to focus on what classes I want to take this year. I'm going to be in AP English of course, as I have been for the last couple years. It's definitely my favorite. I want to take journalism but its going to be hard because they don't let many kids in that class. Our "journalism" is more just propaganda so unless they are sure a kid will be Devout or a Guard, they don't let them take that course. The fact that my dad is a Guard may help, but not necessarily." I shut my journal and took a deep breath.

CHAPTER 4

"Hey, you about ready?" Hearing Allie's voice on the line helped calm my nerves a bit. "Ugh...no. But yeah. How about you guys?" Of course I was never ready for this day. I'd been going to Judgment Day literally my whole life, you'd think I'd be used to it like everyone else. Having Allie with me every single year helped though. Her dad always came by & we all went together every year for the past 6 years once her dad joined the force with my dad. I really don't know what I'd do without her. "We'll be on the way in just a minute. If my BROTHER can get out of the bathroom!" She yelled down the hall & in response her little brother yelled back. "I gotta make sure I look good for the ladies!" I could almost hear her eyes rolling over the phone & I let out a much needed chuckle. "Okay, see you in a bit." "Bye." I hung up the phone, looked in the mirror at my usual attire. I made a special point of not dressing up. A point that my mom hated, which was another reason it brought me my own little bit of satisfaction. A band tee from Black Night Rebellion, jeans, and my beat up combat boots. Looked good to me.

I went down stairs to see if my dad was ready. He was no ordinary spectator, he was a Guard and this year he was on duty. Not working outside the arena like he did on most years. Usually he was just watching over the crowd as they entered to make sure no one got too rowdy but this year was different. This year he was charged with the duty of protecting the Judges family along with 4 other officers.

Judge Bradford was the most powerful man in town. His hair and goatee were nearly all gray but his face was chiseled & distinguished. His eyes were a piercing light blue that held an immense amount of intimidation.

The wolves aged slower than humans and even as they did age they all looked amazing. His wife was fierce & beautiful with long auburn hair and dark green eyes and their son Liam shared his father's eyes & his mothers hair. He looked a lot like both of them and was objectively extremely attractive. Most all the girls in town drooled all over him, even if they didn't stand a chance. I personally couldn't stand him. He was a pompous, rich bully. But for the most part I never saw him even though he was around my age. He stayed far removed from us humans and only hung out with other wolves or maybe a few Devouts on occasion.

I made it down the stairs & quietly peeked around the corner into the kitchen. My dad was sitting in a wooden chair at the round table near the window. I could see the anxiety on his face as he tried to take steady slow breaths. This position was supposed to be one of honor and meant to be a test run for a possible promotion. Only the most trusted of the guards were ever allowed to be around the Judges family. But I could tell he wasn't feeling very honored. I came in and tried to keep things light . "Hey dad." He lifted his head and put on what I could tell was a fake smile. "Hi sweetheart. Are you ready?" I gave him a sympathetic smile. "Yeah I'm ready." Just then I heard the door bell ding and Allie's signature rapid knocks with her long nails. My mom opened the door and smiled warmly. "Hello Robert. Allie, Jake, come in." Allie and her brother smiled, said thank you and came through the door. My mom hugged Uncle Robert's neck. We all stood around talking for a few minutes before getting in our cars & driving to the stadium. Allie would always go with us in our car while her brother went with her dad in theirs. I was grateful to have her to keep me distracted on the drive, but my stomach tightened when we pulled into our parking spot. It was the same routine every year but I was feeling even more anxious than usual this year for some reason. Maybe it was because this year was different because my dad had to go report to security duty for the Judges family. I gave him a quick hug before he left and followed my mom into the stadium. Allie could see the concern and anxiety on my face and gripped my hand. Her warm soft skin helped ease the tension in my jaw a little. "Thanks. I don't know why but I just have…..a bad feeling."

Chapter 5

My dad went to check in with the other officers that were on high security detail as it was called. They walked him to the small but fancy enclosed booth seat that the Judge's family got to sit in. Front & center of course so they could see all the "action". The Guards were charged with watching over the family as they always had adoring fans trying to break into the booth to get a selfie with them. The "festivities", a.k.a trial began & Mrs. Bradford kept getting on to Liam for being on his phone. "Mom. Chill. Its always so boring anyway. Its not like anything exciting is gonna happen. Just a few boring trackers." She rolled her eyes and swept her long beautiful hair aside. "Yes, well, you still need to pay attention. This is what keeps our society running. This is tradition and a part of our history." Liam groaned then smiled a sly grin. "Well I really have to pee. I'm gonna go to the bathroom." His mom tried to stop him but decided it wasn't worth the fight. "Fine, but be quick. And take 2 guards with you." "Why? Everyone is in their seats, no one is gonna mess with me & if they do, I'm a fucking wolf! I can squash these stupid little weak humans." "At least take 1, this is NOT a request!" Liam rolled his eyes. "Whatever." He started to leave the booth, but before he did he pointed to my dad. "You. You're coming with me." My dad bowed his head in respect as was customary when a wolf gave a human a command, and followed close behind. My dad kept a sharp eye out as Liam lazily strolled down the empty halls on the way to the bathroom chatting with one of his friends on his phone. "This year is so boring. There's no executions, just a few stupid trackers. Why the hell do I have to watch this?" They passed a food stand and my dad noticed that someone was ruffling through the trash. It was a Vermin kid. He looked like he'd only been marked maybe a few months ago. My dad knew he'd be ordered to take him in but he hesitated. Liam hadn't noticed yet. If he did go after the Vermin kid, he'd leave Liam unprotected. Not to mention, it was just an 18 year old kid, not much older than his daughter and he was only looking for food. Just then the Vermin kid looked up and saw the two. My dad put a hand on his taser, silently pleading him not to do anything stupid. But his luck ran out and the kid ran straight for them. He slammed into Liam, sending him and his phone flying. They both crashed to the ground and the phone shattered. The kid was laying on his back a few feet from my dad. My dad pointed his taser at him. "Freeze!" The kid scrambled to his feet with his hands up in front of him, shaking in fear. My dad glanced over to Liam who was still laying face down and groaning. "Go!" my dad mouthed to the kid. At first he was unsure, probably thinking it was some sort of trap, but then he took off as fast as he could & turned out of sight. When my dad turned around, he saw Liam sitting up staring at him. "Go get that little Vermin, NOW!" My dad froze, conflicted. "But sir, I'm supposed to be protecting you. I'm not supposed to leave your side." "I said GO. GET. THEM!" My dad grabbed his radio and reported it. "Go get them yourself! By the time they get there, the little Vermin will be gone! Go!" My dad clenched his jaw and tried hard to keep his cadence steady. Though try as he might, he couldn't entirely hide the disdain in his voice. "I'm sorry sir, but its my sworn duty to not leave your side for your safety." "I don't fucking care! Go after them, I order you!" The anger burned a hole through my dad and for a split second he forgot about the massive power imbalance between them. Letting just a hint of his true feelings slip out. "No. I don't give a damn about your order kid, I'm doing my fucking job. You're the one who had to go for a little stroll, I'm not risking everything by chasing after some kid. I'm supposed to stay with you at all times, that's what I'm doing, whether you like it or not." Liam stood up, dusted himself off and winced in pain as he grabbed his hip. He lifted his shirt to see that a large bruise was already forming. Liam stormed off back towards the booth and my dad had to follow behind. When they got there Liam started to go in but then turned to my dad. "No! You stay out here! There are 4 other guards in here, you stay right there." My dad bowed his head and stood outside the door with his arms behind is back. Sweat trickled down his brow as his heart raced. In the booth Liam told is mom everything that happened. Once the Judge was done and came in the booth he told him as well. "I want him executed!" His mother tried to gently talk some reason into him without upsetting him more. "Now Liam, Don't you think that's a little harsh? He was just doing what he was told." "I don't care! He should have gone after that little Vermin! He let him get away on purpose!" "And I told you to take two guards but you refused." Liam lifted his shirt to expose the large, darkening bruise. "Look at what that Vermin did to me. And I'm lucky that's all it was. I wouldn't even need a guard if there weren't those filthy Vermin running around. If he had done his job & arrested him while he was laying there on the ground there'd be one less to worry about. Not to mention the way he fucking talked to me! He may look like a guard, but he damn sure sounded like a Vermin to me!" The Judge thought about it. "One thing is for sure, Redding will never be charged with high security detail again. And a temporary suspension will be in order, but beyond that, I see no cause for further disciplinary action. A few months stuck behind a desk should be sufficient." Liam's face turned red. "What!? You're not even going to place a tracker? " "No Liam. He's not a criminal. He made a decision and in the end he followed his initial orders. He should have arrested the Vermin sooner so it couldn't get away, I agree, but he made the call that we allow them to make. Yes the Vermin got you hurt.." "and broke my phone!" "Yes, and broke your phone, but had he chased after the Vermin, who's to say it wasn't a diversion and another came to take your life? He protected you above all else and that is commendable. I'm already giving him a suspension that may or may not be warranted to satiate you for his disrespect, that is all I feel comfortable doing." Liam plopped back into one of the chairs in the corner, arms crossed. They called in my dad and explained that he would be on 3 months temporary suspension and only allowed to work on paperwork. He bowed his head and breathed a sigh of relief. All the while Liam shot daggers at him with his eyes.

When they released him we were all waiting at the cars. I had to put in my ear buds and listen to my music to calm my nerves. "It shouldn't be taking this long" I told Allie. "Its gonna be ok." Allie said as she hugged my shoulder with one arm and rested her head on mine. A song from BKR pounded in my ears so I didn't hear as my dad walked up. I paused the song & ran up to hug my dad. "What took so long? How did it go?" My dad hugged me tight and smiled but I could tell something was wrong. "I'll tell you in the car sweetheart, let's go." My stomach twisted. If he didn't immediately tell me, that meant something was wrong. Allie got in the backseat of our car with me as she always did. As we pulled out of the parking space my dad was quiet. He waited for a bit until we were on the road to our house to tell us everything that happened. My mom didn't say anything but I couldn't stop myself. "That's ridiculous!" My mom tried to get me to calm down but spoke through gritted teeth. "Christina. Keep it down. Everything is fine." "No its not! He got suspended for doing his job! Or really just because that spoiled brat threw a tantrum over his precious phone getting broken, as if he can't buy 12 more with a snap of his fingers." "Christina! That is enough! The Vermin pose a threat to us all. He was upset, understandably so. His father had a level head and we should be grateful that your father only got three months of desk duty." My dad just gripped the wheel tight and stared at the road. I could hardly believe it. Was mom actually defending that asshole? Was she actually mad at my dad for just doing what he was told? I wanted to say something but Allie squeezed my arm and I sunk back into my seat and kept my mouth shut. When we got home I had to say bye to Allie. I hugged her tight for as long as I could, then let go and waved, reluctantly closing the door. My mom tried to talk to me but I just sprinted upstairs, took my earbuds out of my pocket, put them in my ears & blasted my song as I fell back onto my bed. The words helped calm me down as I sang them quietly to myself, resonating with them on a very deep level. "Please hear my silent cries, see the pain in my eyes. Hear the screams coming from within, as I plaster on a happy grin, being crushed by the weight of what I hide. I'm dying on the inside. But you'll never know cuz you don't look deep enough to see. Making you believe I'm ok is killing me..."

CHAPTER 6

It was the first day of school. Oh boy. I shoved the last of my stuff in my dark camo backpack, grabbed my keys and ran downstairs as my mom called for me from the living room. I got down stairs, ignored the dirty look from my mom, kissed my dad on the cheek as he finished getting dressed for work and rushed out the door.

When I pulled into the parking spot in front of the school, my stomach started doing flips. But just then Allie pulled up beside me in her little blue car. It was a lot newer and more sleek than my faded black truck but I loved this truck. It was a 16th birthday present from my dad. I got out & said hi to Allie. She looked a lot more excited than I was. "Seniors at last, can you believe it?" "Yeah I can't wait to be done with all this." She playfully shoved into my shoulder. "Come on, cheer up. I know you're stressed out, and I'm here for you, you know that, but this is gonna be great. You gotta believe it." I shook my head and tried to smile. "You're right. Let's go." Most of the morning went by fairly fast. Pretty standard stuff.

At lunch I went to my locker only to find Blair standing in front of it. Apparently my locker was just a couple doors down from her boyfriend Matt's and she was waiting for him to put his stuff away. She was, of course dressed in a purple shirt and purple plaid skirt with a matching headband in her hair. I stood there waiting impatiently for her to stop flirting with Matt and get out of the way.

She noticed my foot tapping and looked over, giving a sneer. "What do you want?" I felt the anger start to bubble up. "You're in front of my locker." "Boo hoo, you can wait." I was trying not to loose my cool when she looked again and got a surprised look on her face. "Wait, you're Christina Redding. Your dad nearly got Liam Bradford killed." Matt finally turned around, as did his friend Cory who was standing on the other side of him. "Oh fuck! That was your dad? Shit, I'd move if I were you." I was just about to lose it when Allie put her hand on my shoulder. "Her dad followed his orders and protected Liam." Blair laughed, rolling her eyes. "Yeah well that's not what everyone is saying. He let a nasty little Vermin hurt Liam and then let it get away." I was so furious that all I could do is lower my head, close my eyes and grit my teeth. My fists were clenched at my sides so tightly that even my short nails were digging into my palm. Allie spoke up for me, knowing that if I said anything I'd probably scream and throw a punch. "Yeah well I don't care what everyone is saying, they're wrong, now move!" Blair rolled her eyes again, something that seemed like her favorite thing to do, and moved aside. "Whatever. Come on Matt, let's go." Her, Matt and Cory all walked off towards the exit. I muttered "Thanks" between my clenched jaws & opened my locker. I put my books away and grabbed my keys.

Allie just sat and listened in the passenger seat of my truck as I ranted. "That bitch! You know it was probably her that started the rumors. How dare she say that shit about my dad! She thinks she's some sort of Devout Princess that can do whatever the hell she wants. I think the only person that's a bigger spoiled brat is that pompous wolf Liam. Everyone is so concerned about him when all he did was throw a temper tantrum to his mommy and daddy. Its fucking ridiculous!" Allie tried to be the voice of reason, as usual. "She is a bitch. Her and her whole little cult of followers. But we both know that everything they say is shit. And they want to piss you off. They want you to get mad and scream and yell cuz they're nothing but over grown schoolyard bullies. I know its hard to just ignore them, but if you can keep your cool, they'll eventually move on to bigger prey." I took a deep breath. "I know. You're right…..again. And thanks for helping me back there. I was so close to taking a swing at her." Allie laughed. "I know, I could tell. But I wasn't about to let you get suspended, or worse on your first day. Then who would I go to lunch with?" We both laughed as I pulled into the pizza place.

After shoving the last piece of thin crust pizza in my mouth, we headed back. I just tried to keep my head down and get through the rest of the day in peace.

Chapter 7

I took a seat in my last period class. Economics. I figured it would be about something super boring but when the teacher started talking, my ears immediately perked up and I started paying attention. "What is the economic impact of the Vermin?" He started talking about the different classes and how they benefit our economy and all the same stuff I had heard a million times but then started delving more in to the Vermin and my curiosity was piqued. "The Vermin are supposed to remain exiled from our cities and thusly have little impact on our economy and daily lives, but this isn't always the case. At times they leave behind belongings in the sewers that our city maintenance teams need to remove. Worst still is when they do venture into the city to steal food or personal property. This creates a loss for the businesses that have been stolen from and raises prices overall. Studies are being conducted to determine the actual yearly average economic impact of this theft, but it could be as much as tens of thousands of dollars." When the bell rang I slowly put all of my things in my backpack and waited for everyone to file out of the room. When everyone else was gone, I went up to the teachers desk. He stopped moving around papers to look at me. "Yes, miss... Redding, is it?" He asked as he looked down at me through his little square glasses that were perched at the end of his nose. I cleared my throat, feeling nervous and intimidated. "Um...yes, I had a question.

Where could I possibly learn more about what we were talking about in class? Like, with the Vermin?" He gave me a skeptical look and my heart started pounding faster. "I wouldn't have thought you would've been interested in something like that." I shuffled my feet a bit, thinking fast. "Yeah its just, with my dad being a guard and all, its kind of expected that I'll be a cop when I grow up and with everything that happened at the Stadium, I want to learn more so I can predict their behavior and make sure that something like that never happens to me." He thought about it for a second then relaxed a bit and seemed satisfied with that answer. "I see. That makes sense. I'm proud of you for being proactive. There aren't many places you can research such things, but there's a few books in the library you could check out." He scribbled a few names on a piece of paper then he handed it to me. "Here, take this to the librarian." He got a big smile & blushed a little. "And, tell her I sent you." I smiled and took the paper, trying not to make it obvious that I was internally gagging at the thought of the two of them flirting.

I quickly headed to the library and went up to the desk where the librarian was checking in some books. "Excuse me?" I said, startling her accidentally. "Oh, sorry." I said. She slowed her breathing & tugged a little at her button down pale blue shirt. "No, no, its ok. Shouldn't you be headed home?" "Yes, but I wanted to see if I could check out these books real quick." I handed the piece of paper to her and tried not to sweat as she unfolded it and looked over it closely. "Hhhmmm, these are some…unconventional books." I shifted the weight in my backpack, trying to act as calm as possible. "Yeah, Mr. Williams said you'd be able to help me out." She raised her eyebrows and blushed a little. "Oh, well, if Mr. Williams approved of it, then I suppose its alright." I smiled, trying again to not gag. She typed on the computer then went off to a shelf towards the back of the library. After a couple minutes she came back holding three thin books. She scanned them into the computer then asked for my student ID card. I pulled the badge that dangled from a red lanyard off my neck and handed it to her. She scanned it and handed it back to me along with the books. I took the books from her outstretched hand. "Thank you." She smiled and waved then got back to doing what she was doing before. I clutched them to my chest and walked out to my truck as fast as possible. Luckily there weren't many students left so no one really noticed. When I got to my truck I was finally able to relax a little. I jumped though when I heard my phone ding. It was a text from Allie. "Hey. I had to head home, I'll talk to you later." I texted back real quick. "Yeah sorry, I had to get some books for an assignment. Talk to you here in a bit." Then I put my phone in the passenger seat & looked at the books for the first time. A dark green book with the title "The Forth Class" in dingy yellow letters. A reddish orange book with dark brown letters that said, "The History And Impact of The Vermin". And a light gray book with, "The Inner Workings of The Vermin Class and how to Eradicate Them" written in black letters. I put them in my backpack and started the truck, heading home. When I got home my mom tried to ask how my day went. I didn't pay much attention to her and just said "It was fine" as I went straight upstairs to my room and closed the door.

I pulled the books out of my backpack and laid on my bed with them. I started with the orange book but it seemed to be mostly all of the same things that Mr. Williams talked about in class. I tossed it aside and grabbed the green book. "In our society there are 3 main classes, The Devout, The Guard, And The Neutral classes. However there is a fourth class known as The Vermin. This is a class of humans that few will ever see." This wasn't anything new to me, again, we're taught this stuff from kindergarten. I was getting bored so I closed it and picked up the gray book. The others were educational but I noticed right away that this one seemed different. It started with such hatred and vitriol. "The Vermin are a class of humans who seek anarchy and the destruction of our civilized society. They need to be eradicated from our cities as much as possible. Originally, they were kept alive as a show of mercy to their families in order to keep the peace, but those days are behind us as they become more and more emboldened and pose a greater risk. The time has come to exterminate them entirely. For many years our leaders have been trying to reduce their numbers but their brave efforts seem to have little impact. Sterilization has helped keep them in check, but more end up being marked every day. No one is sure yet if it is due to a random genetic mutation or due to radicalization in childhood but researchers are hard at work to determine the cause. Currently it appears to be a bit of both. This is why it is increasingly important to discourage any discussion of The Vermin in any other form other than a negative light and to uphold the values of the family and moral social norms. The Guard must capture any Vermin found for imprisonment and execution so that their numbers can begin to decrease. With the deterrence of execution, hopefully less and less humans will be swayed and marked as Vermin. Any citizen that sees a Vermin is required by law, and moral duty to report it to The Guard so that they may be captured. Only with the help of every citizen can we finally truly eradicate the threat that is this radical and violent class of humans." I slammed the book closed and threw it off my bed. A tear rolled down my cheek. "Eradicated?" I whispered to myself. I knew that they were sometimes executed, but it was so common place that few people ever really talked about it. It shouldn't have been a shock to me, but it was. They were talking about human beings like some sort of insect that needed to be exterminated. We all live in this reality and are taught from birth that this is just how it is, so we never really think about it, never question it. For the first real time my eyes were opened and it hit me in the chest like a massive punch, knocking the wind out of me. I had to know what it was like down there, where they lived. I started making a plan. Unfortunately I would have to wait for little while until I could get up the nerve but I was determined.

CHAPTER 8

———————

I spent the next couple of weeks keeping my head down, trying to act as normal as I could, to not make waves. I wanted to tell Allie about my plan, about what I read, all of my thoughts and feelings, just as I did with everything else, but I figured it would be better if I didn't. The less she knew the better because I couldn't bare it if I got her in any trouble. So for her safety I kept it all to myself. Several times I thought about calling off my plans, but the words from the book kept playing in my head and I decided I'd do it, I just had to wait for the right time.

Finally the weekend came and I was ready. Friday I laid the foundation by mentioning to Allie that I didn't feel well after lunch. I kept acting more and more tired and lethargic until the end of the day. In my last period I asked to go to the nurse. I told the nurse that my stomach was hurting and I was nauseous. "I think it may have been something I ate." She looked me over than asked if I wanted to leave early or wait the last 30 minutes until the final bell. I said that I would really like to go ahead and leave so I didn't have to fight the crowds and traffic jams to get home. "Okay, I'll let the front desk know. Feel better." I waved weakly and said, "Thank you." I walked slowly out of the school and to my truck, hunched over and holding my stomach. When I got in the truck I texted Allie. "Going home a little early. My stomach's really hurting, gonna go take a long nap and try to feel better." Then I texted my mom basically the same thing. They both texted back quickly with some version of "Okay, hope you feel better". When I got home I went upstairs and shut the door. Then I started setting my plan into motion. I emptied out my backpack and started putting in things I had been stashing all week and had hidden in a secret space behind my head board. A few little bags of chips, a couple bottles of water, a small first-aid kit that I had put together, and a flashlight. I went to my closet and grabbed a pair of my old tennis shoes that I wouldn't mind getting dirty and some old clothes that had some holes. I put on the clothes and put my pajamas over them. The shoes I shoved into my backpack. I put my baseball cap and green hoodie in there as well and, with a little effort, zipped it up. I wished I could bring more, but that was all I could carry. Lastly I grabbed the knife that my dad had given me for my birthday last year. It was a folding knife but rather large with a dark wood handle. On the blade was engraved some lettering. "I'll always keep you safe." Something he use to say to me when I was a kid and would wake up from a nightmare, which was pretty often. I ran my finger over the words, smiled, then folded it and put it in my pocket.

Just then there was a knock on the door and my heart pounded. I shoved my backpack aside, jumped into bed and pulled my blanket over me. "Come in." My dad slowly poked his head in. "Hey sweetheart. How are you feeling?" I gave him a sad little smile. "Not great. I'm really tired mostly." He gave me a sympathetic look. "Okay baby, well get your rest." I smiled & he closed the door. "That was close." I thought after the door clicked. I looked at the clock on my phone. 5:26. I had to wait until it was dark so I had to keep my mind busy for another three hours. This was not going to be easy. I put in my ear buds and listened to some music while drawing in my sketch pad.

After what seemed like forever, the sun was finally down. My mom had offered me some food but I told her I couldn't eat right now and just wanted to sleep. Luckily she left me alone after that. I peeled off my pajamas to reveal my old clothes underneath. Before opening my window, I hesitated. What if I got caught? The only other time I had snuck out was when Allie and I tried to go to a friend's party last year and we both got caught. We got in so much trouble, and that was nothing compared to this. My gaze fell onto the light gray book still sitting on the floor, halfway under my bed, and all doubt vaporized. Taking a deep steadying breath I slowly and carefully raised the window, and felt the cool breeze rush in. My feet carefully tapped the eve of the house, searching for a secure footing. Once I felt sure that I wouldn't somehow fall off the roof and break my back, I climbed out, then over to the side of the house where I lowered myself down to the cinderblock fence. With a light "oof" I jumped down and landed on the cool grass. I looked around, half expecting to see cops or wolves coming to arrest me. Luckily, because just about no one ever broke city curfew, the street was completely empty and eerily quiet. "I did it." I thought to myself smiling as a rush of adrenaline coursed through me. But I couldn't celebrate long because I had to do what I came to do and get back before anyone noticed. I reached into my backpack and grabbed my baseball cap and my hoodie, putting both of them on, along with the tennis shoes. Then I zipped up the backpack and slung it onto my shoulder. It was then that I realized I had no real idea where I was going. With a bit of a lump in my throat I just decided to start walking, hoping that I'd figure it out soon. I walked back to the alley and just kept walking, trying to stay in the shadows as much as possible. It seemed like I had been walking for hours but when I checked my phone, it had only been about forty five minutes. I came to a main street and saw what I had been searching for. A manhole cover. When I tried to lift it, I realized that it was much heavier than I had anticipated. I thanked myself for remembering to sneak a crowbar from my truck into my sleeve when I came home. I pulled it out of my backpack and, with a great deal of sweat and muffled grunting, I pried the cover up and slid it over just enough for me to slip down into the hole. I slowly started down the dark & wet ladder, stopping to slide the cover back in place. When I did, all light vanished and I had to navigate my way down in complete darkness. Once I felt hard ground beneath my feet I let go of the ladder and pulled out my flashlight. The beam of light illuminated the raised walking paths on either side of a flowing, stinking river of black water. I covered my nose with the sleeve of my hoodie and walked forward.

CHAPTER 9

"Maybe this was a mistake." I thought as I checked my phone. I had been walking for close to an hour and hadn't found anything. Then I heard whispers down a tunnel that led off to the right. As I followed the sound it got louder. "Hello?" I called into the dark tunnel. Just beyond the reach of my flashlight a voice called back. "Go away! We're not doing anything! Please, just let us go!" "It's ok! I'm not here to hurt you or turn you in. I just want to talk." Another voice echoed through the tunnel this time. "I don't believe you! Go the fuck away!" "Please, I swear, I'm not one of them, I just want to talk." A few more whispers then two people stepped into the beam of light. One was a guy that I recognized as a guy from school that I shared a couple classes with last year. I thought he had moved away at the start of this year. And the other was a woman that looked to be in her 20s. "I promise, I'm not one of them." The woman narrowed her eyes. "Then why are you down here?" I shuffled my feet nervously, trying to figure out the right thing to say. "I...I just need to know what its like down here. I've been reading things and....I just can't believe how bad things are. We're all told, but I had to see it for myself." The guy seemed to relax but the woman still looked at me with obvious suspicion & disgust. "So what, you just got bored & wanted to gawk at the poor little Vermin? Well We're not some animals in a zoo for you to laugh at or pity before going home to your comfy bed." "No, I promise, its not like that! I hate the wolves. I've started seeing just how bad they are & I want to write it all down so I can get it out someday so more people can know. Again, we all know but no one really thinks about it. They're desensitized to it. I want to show people that real, innocent human beings are being put through hell for no damn reason. Maybe someday that could turn things around." The woman scoffed but I continued. "Or maybe it won't change anyone's mind, but its still something I just felt like I needed to do. I'm just trying to help, I promise. But I get it, I can go if you don't want me here." "Well, we don't." I turned to leave but the guy stopped me. "Wait! At least tell us your name." I turned back around. "Christina Redding." He smiled shyly. "I'm Marcos. This is Daniella." "Dani." She corrected him. I smiled back at him & gave a quick little wave. "Hi Marcos, hi Dani. Nice to meet you." Marcos whispered in Dani's ear real quick. She looked annoyed and whispered back. After a minute of back and forth he got a big grin. "Christina, would you like to talk for a little while?" I felt a flutter of hope again and smiled. "Yeah, I'd love that!" He gestured for me to come closer & we walked a short way together to a spot that was a little cleaner with cardboard laid on the ground and they sat down. I followed, looking around with my flashlight at the dark, dirty surroundings.

Marcos spoke first. "Sorry for Dani, we hardly ever see people and when we do....well....." He trailed off and glanced at her. It was then that I noticed that, other than the smudges of dirt and who knows what else that they both had all over, she also had some bad bruises on her arms that looked like hand prints. She caught me looking & sneered. "Yeah, that's right little girl. What do you think happens when a guy from up there sees a Vermin woman? You think they're polite? No. They do whatever the fuck they want. Its not like they gotta worry about anything. We can't go to the cops. We can't have babies. They can do whatever the fuck they want and get away with it." My stomach twisted in knots as I understood what she meant. "I....I never thought of that. I'm so sorry!" She shifted her weight and while she still looked angry, I could see the pain in her eyes that she was trying so hard to hide. "Yeah well, it happens.

There's nothing we can do. Sometimes we get a beating after, just for the hell of it. But that's if we're lucky. The ones who aren't, get turned over to the cops or worse. Marcos is lucky that he's only been down here for a couple of weeks. He wasn't here when this happened to me this time around so he didn't get caught. We only met up a few days ago. But down here, you stick together. You can go months without seeing anyone other than slimy Devouts or Guards that just wanna take you or hurt you. So when we find another of our kind we try to stay together." I bit my cheek hoping what I said next wouldn't offend her or upset her. "I get it. I mean, obviously I can't fully understand, by any means, but I understand more now than I did. I know you have to hate pretty much everyone up there, but I can say at least all Guards aren't bad. My dad is a Guard. He hates the wolves just like I do. He just doesn't want to get anyone hurt. The other day, at Judgment Day, he was protecting that fucking asshole Liam, the Judge's son. A Vermin guy not much older than me ran at them & Liam insisted that he go after him but my dad refused. He said he was just doing his job and staying with Liam but I know its because he didn't wanna turn in that kid." Marcos got a big smile. "Hey that was Eli! He told us about that! He just knew he was done for. I told him he was an idiot for charging them like that but he said he panicked and didn't really think about it."

We talked for a while about what it was like down there. "Why do you guys stay down here? Wouldn't it be easier in the woods?" Dani chuckled. "Oh, yeah, its so much better. Little girl you have no idea. You have to catch and kill your own food, you have to make your own shelter and hope it can keep you warm enough, and hidden enough. And there's these guys who call themselves hunters. Some are wolves but most are slimy Devouts. They go out in the woods and try to hunt down any Vermin that's out there. We get beat up down here from time to time, but out there? They get.....well, let's just say kid, you don't wanna know." She shuddered and clutched her knees tight. Marcos rested his head on her shoulder. "Dani's twin sister decided to go out there. Dani went after her and witnessed a bunch of hunters....well......." A tear rolled down her cheek but she sat up and looked me right in the eye. "They slaughtered her." Marcos tried to pull her back a little but she brushed him off. "No, she wanted to know, she needs to know. It won't make a difference, but she asked for it. When they were done...having their way with her they slit her throat and strung her up like a damn deer. They laughed and threw beer in her face while she bled out. They stayed there for a long time after she was dead, then left her there strung up to leave some sort of message. I had to hide the whole time so they wouldn't catch me. When I was sure they were gone I went and got her down. I didn't have any way to dig her a grave but I did my best to cover her body so people wouldn't see her like that. I'm sure animals got her though. That was 6 years ago. And that's not even the most messed up thing I've seen." I had closed my eyes tight but tears still snuck out. My stomach was so twisted up that I felt like I might throw up. I took a few deep breaths and looked at her with a new appreciation for all she had been through. "I.....I.I'm so sorry! That's horrible!" She wiped a tear away as quickly as she could. "Yeah well, you wanted to know what its like as a Vermin, why we choose to stay here." She stuck out her wrist and there were several jagged scars. "I tried to do it. I couldn't live this way. But I met some others and they kept me going. Now I'm trying to do that for Marcos. Some days I don't really know why I'm trying so hard to survive, but we're like a family down here. We look out for each other."

I sat there in silence for a moment, trying to gather my thoughts. Before I could say anything I heard footsteps of someone running towards us from the darkness and heard a woman's voice. "Dani, they're getting worse, you have to get back." Dani got up quickly and ran in the direction the voice had come from. Marcos got up but he seemed conflicted on whether to follow or not. He finally turned and ran after her, seeming surprised when I came with him. We ran for a while until we reached a spot with a couple of makeshift tents. A man was standing outside the tent pacing but looked relieved when we ran up. "You're here. Who is...whatever, just help them." We all went inside the tent made mostly of sheets and blankets and there on the floor were laying a man and woman. The woman looked close to my age and the man looked a little older than Dani. Both of their faces were twisted in pain, but they stayed silent. They both had slashes on their arms that were poorly wrapped up with torn fabric and scratched all over. "Wh....what happened?" I said and Dani realized for the first time that I had followed them. "What the hell are you still doing here? Go home to your cozy little life." "I want to help. What the hell happened to them?" The woman who had brought us there spoke up. "Wolves. They like to use us for their little play things. They come down here sometimes in wolf form to attack us....to.........devour us." I could hardly believe what she was saying. "Wait...you mean...they, they....eat people?" "Yes." I covered my mouth to stop the acid that was rising in my throat. I tried to not to gag as I spoke. "Ho...how do people not know about this? How have they not been caught" "They're wolves, they write the laws, they control the people who enforce the laws, they can get away with whatever the hell they want & make people think whatever they want. Its one of their many dirty little secrets. Out in the woods they pay hunters to track us down so they don't have to be seen doing it themselves. Sometimes they just kill whoever they catch..." she paused glancing in Dani's direction. Dani winced but the woman continued with a sympathetic look on her face. "Sometimes they catch us and turn us over to the cops, but sometimes they give them over to the wolves. Down here, they won't be seen, but they don't like being down here, don't wanna get dirty I guess. So it's not that often, but when they do it's.....horrific. These two just barely escaped but they got hurt pretty bad." I slid off my backpack and dug anything out I could. "Here, take these. I know its not much, but it's all I have." I handed them the bag of chips and bottles of water. But it was when I pulled out the first aid kit that they got really excited. The woman took it and then gave me a short hug. "Thank you so much! Getting our hands on stuff like this is hard. Very hard. That's what Dani and Marcos were going to do was trying to find something to help." "Its just some bandages, some alcohol pads, stuff like that. Oh, but there is a bottle of pain pills in there. They're just over the counter but they should help with the pain. I just wish I could do more." The woman smiled warmly. "No, you have no idea how much this helps. Thank you." She turned to tend to the two on the floor. I wanted so badly to do something more to help, but just then my back pocket buzzed. It was the alarm on my phone. "Shit, I gotta get back before my parents realize I'm gone. Thank you for talking to me. Maybe, just maybe we can make people see how bad it is and make a difference. Maybe not, but I'm gonna try." "No problem. Thank you so much for your help. I hope what you write really can make things change." Marcos shook my hand. Dani just crossed her arms. "It won't. Nothing ever changes. Thanks for the help, now get back before you end up causing more trouble for us. If you look at the wall, there's arrows that will get you back to up top. Let's go Marcos." She turned and started to walk over to the other woman who knelt down by the ones on the floor. Marcos walked to the wall real quick and pointed. When I shined my flashlight on the brick and concrete wall I saw a faded black arrow that looked like it had been drawn in chalk. Then he gave me a quick smile and turned to stand behind Dani. I walked in the direction of the arrow and in several feet, I saw another one, then another one. After a while I found the ladder I had climbed down. Before climbing back up I glanced back, hoping that they would all be ok. I very carefully pushed open the heavy cover and peeked outside. I didn't see anyone so I quickly crawled out and replaced the cover.

CHAPTER 10

The sky was still dark, but growing lighter so I checked my phone. 5:53 am. The sun would be coming up in less than an hour which meant that cops would be starting to patrol the streets. Running back as fast as I could, I tried to stay in the shadows. I finally got back to my house but before I climbed back up on the fence I tried to catch my breath for a second. But I couldn't take long because I had to get back in my bed before anyone noticed I was gone. I scrambled up the fence and cautiously tip toed out onto the eve of the house. My teeth clenched as I opened up my window, cringing at the squeak it made, hoping no one heard. The sun was just starting to peek above the horizon and I heard a cop car coming down the street next to ours, about to turn down our street. After stepping back into my room as quietly as I could, I shut the window and closed the curtains just before the cop car drove by our house. My backpack slipped off my shoulder & I changed my clothes real quick, threw my hat and backpack into the closet and got into bed. It felt like it was no more than a few minutes before my mom knocked on my door but my alarm clock said it was 9:25. "Christina? How are you feeling?" She said through the door. "A little better, just tired." "Ok, I'll let you rest. If you want anything for breakfast just let me know." I muttered, "Okay, thank you." and rolled back over in bed. No matter how much I tried not to, I couldn't help but think about everything I had seen and heard down there. Images flashed in my mind that I wish so bad would just go away. "But she was right. I asked for it. I went down there on my own, knowing it was gonna be bad." Even though the images tried their best to keep me awake, sleep finally won.

Suddenly I was in the woods. All around me I heard men laughing and leaves crunching under heavy hunting boots. I ran as fast as I could but it felt like I was running through sand. I silently pleaded my muscles to work harder and to go faster but they refused. As the laughing got louder and louder, it was now accompanied by a fierce growling. "Look at this one Jim. She's a young one. This is gonna be fun." I heard the men just behind me and felt a heavy hand grip my neck from behind as it pulled me to the ground. My eyes slammed shut, but when I opened them I was in my bed, breathing heavily. My clock read 11:47. I stretched, rubbed my face, then got up and got dressed. When I came down stairs to the kitchen my mom was sitting at the table reading as she did a lot. "Oh, how are you feeling? Are you hungry yet?" I grumbled and yawned before replying. "Yeah I'm just gonna grab something quick though. I feel a lot better but I'm sill pretty tired so I'll probably just write in my room today. I have an essay due on Monday." "Okay. Well if you need anything let me know." She went right back to her book as I grabbed some snacks out of the pantry and went back up to my room. While I climbed the stairs I thought to myself, "yeah, as if you really care." I did write for the rest of the day, but not an essay for school. I wrote down as many details from my trip to the sewers as I could remember, which was pretty much everything. That experience was burned into my memory whether I wanted it to be or not. But writing it down helped. I made sure to put it all down in ink and on my laptop, just in case.

It was so hard to act like everything was normal after that. I told my mom I was fine to go back to school when she asked the next day. "Yeah, obviously it was just something I ate. I'll be fine by tomorrow." I had to go to school pretending I hadn't learned the most heart wrenching, most horrifying things I had ever heard over the weekend. But, little did I know what was going on with Liam was so much worse.

CHAPTER 11

Liam had spent his whole weekend ranting to his friends about how much he hated my dad. "That fucking Guard! All of this is his fucking fault! If he would have just stopped that stupid little Vermin before he ran at me, I wouldn't have gotten hurt, my phone wouldn't have gotten smashed, none of it. Then he wouldn't even chase after him! I bet he wanted him to get away. And then the way he talked me. Who the fuck does that asshole think he is? I can't believe my dad let him go!" "Maybe we should do something about that." One of his wolf friends said as he drug his thumb across his neck. The four of his other friends laughed but Liam didn't. He just smiled and said, "Just a minute, I gotta make a call." He pulled out the shiny new phone his mom had bought and dialed a number as he walked off from his friends.

CHAPTER 12

It was Wednesday already but it was getting harder to put aside the thoughts about being down in the sewers. Every night I wrote about it in my journal, making sure to write down everything I could remember. I still wasn't really sure what I was going to do with it, but I figured the best place to start would be Allie. "Maybe she knows someone who could do something." I thought to myself. But in all reality, I just really needed to talk to my best friend about everything. I couldn't keep this all to myself any more. I called her and told her to meet me a little early before school. When we got parked in our spots at the school it was still early enough that no one was really there. I had her get in my truck to talk to her about it. I told her most everything, sparing her from some of the more traumatic details. She just sat there in stunned silence until I was done. "What....what the fuck were you thinking? Christina, you could have been caught, or worse, you could've gotten yourself killed!" I gripped the steering wheel and just looked straight ahead as I talked. "I know, I know. It was a dumb move. But I had to know. We all know its bad down there, but its so much worse than you think. They tell us about this stuff from the minute we get into school and just act like its no big deal. They desensitize us to it so we don't even question it. But Allie, they aren't Vermin, they're human beings. People we went to school with. Someone has to do something." Allie tried to gather her thoughts but it wasn't doing much good. "Like what? Start some sort of revolution?" "Maybe." I said finally turning to look her in the eye. "Why not? They did it. Why can't we?" "Be..because we're not wolves. We don't have that kind of power. People would just get killed, innocent people. Just to prove a point. You said it yourself, they can get away with anything they want." I took a deep breath and tried to sound more reasonable. "I know. And its not like I'm saying we can overthrow our whole society by ourselves or anything, but we do outnumber them. If we could get enough people to stand up, maybe we could do something meaningful. The way the Vermin are treated, this whole fucking class system, Judgement Day, its all just so twisted and horrible. Something has to change. And it has to start somewhere." She thought for a second, choosing her words before she spoke again. "You're right, something does have to change. That's all so....horrible! But Christina, our Birthdays are in a few weeks. And we're going to be marked. Even if you don't get marked as a Vermin, if they catch you doing anything against the wolves, even talking badly about them, they'll say you're a Vermin & take you away. I...I don't want you to be one of those people down there fighting for your life, trying not to get eaten." I winced at the thought. "I know. I've been thinking about that." There was a couple minutes of silence. "Listen. The BKR concert is in three days. We worked so hard to get those tickets. All of this can wait a few more days. Let's just go to the concert, have the time of our lives, then we can worry about all this, deal?" I thought to myself, "True, and this is probably the last time I'll get to have fun before being marked as a Vermin and thrown in the sewer, or worse." I gave an only halfway sincere smile and relaxed the tension in my shoulders. "Yeah, I guess you're right. This can wait."

CHAPTER 13

Three days later I put on my cutest cropped BKR tee, jeans & attempted my best at a dark smoky eye. One of the very few times I wore makeup. When I heard the door bell I ran downstairs to open the door for Allie. She squealed when she saw me & we hugged. My mom gave me a stern look. "Please be careful. You know how these types of concerts can be". She said with a significant amount of disdain. My dad came up laughing with his arms out for a hug, which I gladly accepted. "Oh leave the girls alone. They'll be fine. I'll be outside patrolling the perimeter, nothing will happen to them. Just keep an eye out and never leave a drink unattended, got it?" I smiled and nodded, as did Allie. "Yes sir" we said in unison. My dad gave me a big kiss on the cheek and laughed. "Alright, well you girls get going. I'll be headed there shortly after you." "Okay. Love you dad!" We hurried to get in my truck and blasted BKR songs the whole way there. When we got to the stadium I stood for just a second to admire it. We went here every year but now it looked like an entirely different place. Instead of a cold celebration of death bathed in hot summer sunlight, now it was surrounded by cool night air as colorful lights danced all around. There were just as many people as there always were, but the whole energy felt different. We got in line and when we finally got to the front entrance they scanned our tickets and let us inside. It was a lot more chaotic than what I was used to when we usually came here, but I didn't mind at all. We couldn't push through people to get the best seats, but it didn't matter because the huge screens made it feel like we were right up next to the stage. Allie and I screamed and cheered after every one of the opening bands finished their set, not because we love the band but because it meant we were one step closer to seeing the best band ever formed. After a while the stage went dark. When the lights came back on he was standing there on stage and his face was up close on the large screens. Shoulder length jet black hair, soft blue eyes, a blood red guitar in one hand, the microphone in another. I felt my heart skip a beat. Sure, I might of felt like I was being juvenile. Like a 12 year old with a crush, but I didn't care. "Hey, I'm Caleb Knight and we are Black Knight Rebellion, how are you guys doing tonight?" The whole stadium erupted in roaring cheers. "What was that? I didn't quite hear you?" I didn't think it was possible to get louder, but somehow we all did. I would probably loose my voice if I kept this up but it was a small sacrifice for this moment. "Yeah! Let's go!" They started playing & were every bit as amazing as they were in their recordings. Allie and I sang along to every word.

Chapter 14

Meanwhile, my dad was out patrolling the perimeter fence with another officer. "I hate working nights like this. Nothing more than a few drunken idiot teenagers. I'm bored as hell." My dad laughed. "Yeah I know what you mean. But weren't you the one who volunteered for this post Pierce?" Pierce laughed. "Well, yeah just because I needed the hours. Still sucks though." He checked his phone real quick then put it back in his pocket. "At least there's not too much longer. But hey, I'm starving, I'm gonna go grab some grub, you want anything?" My dad smiled. "Yeah. Grab me a hotdog." Pierce nodded as he walked off towards the stadium and the food trucks that surrounded it. "Will do. Be back in a sec." Shortly after my dad was left alone he heard a noise back in the darkest part of the fence to the side of the stadium. He walked over with a hand on his taser and another holding his flashlight. "Security, who's there?" A man stepped out of the shadows. He was tall, muscular, had long hair that was pulled back in a ponytail and a goatee. He was clearly in his late twenties but didn't have a mark on his hand, meaning he was a wolf. My dad took his hand off his taser and relaxed a bit. "Oh, excuse me sir. But I will need to ask you to vacate this area." The man smiled as he started walking toward my dad, acting as though he was going to leave. "Of course, officer." But when he got to my dad he suddenly grabbed onto him from behind, pulling his arms behind his back. Because he was a wolf, he was much stronger than my dad and able to keep him still. The wolf ripped my dads radio off its clip and tossed it hard so it went skidding off into the dark. He pulled out a big knife and sank it into my dads chest. He then let go and shoved my dad, face first into the hard asphalt and took off. A couple minutes later Pierce came back holding two hotdogs. "Jack? Where'd you go?" When he saw my dads feet laying in the shadows he dropped the hot dogs and ran to him. "Jack!? Jack!" he got to his side and knelt down while grabbing his radio and pressed the button. "Officer down! Officer down! We need medical assistance to the Southeast side of the perimeter fence, now!" My dad tried to say something but he was too weak as he took fast and shallow breaths. "Its ok Jack, just hold on." But just as the medical team began to run up to them, my dad took his final breath. Pierce sat there for a moment, in the pool of blood with shock and horror on his face. He pulled his phone out and looked at the last text. "Go get something to eat." He stepped aside for the medical team and paced back and forth, gripping the back of his head thinking to himself. "What the fuck have I done? They didn't say this is what they were planning! Jack, I'm so, so sorry. No amount of money is worth this."

Chapter 15

Inside there seemed to be a big commotion and someone ran up on stage to whisper in Caleb's ear while he finished up a song. On the big screens I could see the look on Caleb's face but he was clearly trying to hide it. He nodded as the man left the stage. "Cut it guys", he said to the rest of the band, then he spoke to the audience. "Hey guys, you've been amazing, but it looks like we gotta cut the show a little short." There were groans of disappointment from everyone in the stadium. "I know, I know, but hey, if you go to the BKR experience dot com and email us the number on your ticket, we'll send a free signed copy of our latest album, how about that?" Everyone seemed pretty pleased with his proposal but I had the darkest, most sinking feeling I had ever had. "So we ask that everyone please exit as calmly as possible. The security guards will escort you out, and have a great night everyone." With that he turned to talk to the band and everyone started to leave. "I wonder what happened?" I had almost forgotten that Allie was there so I jumped a little. "Oh, I...I don't know, but it couldn't have been good. Let's go." We made our way through the sea of people, being pushed and shoved like sheep being herded into a slaughter pen. When we got close to the main entrance I saw my Uncle Robert, Allie's dad standing talking to one of the Guards in plain clothes. He caught my eye and made his way through to me and Allie. "Girls, there you are." "Dad? What are you doing here? I thought it was your night off?" "Hey Allie cat. Yeah…it….it was. But they called me up here. Listen, girls, I have to tell you something…." He trailed off, obviously not sure how to say what he needed to say. But he didn't have to. I could tell by the look on his face alone. "Tell me what happened to my dad." When he stumbled over his words, trying to find a way to lessen the blow, I clenched my fists while tears already started to tumble from my eyes. "What happened to my dad! I'm not five, tell me what fucking happened to my dad!" He took a deep breath and nodded. "He…he was stabbed in the heart. He didn't make it. I'm so sorry Christina." And just like that, all of the oxygen in the entire stadium seemed to vanish. My head began to spin and the crowd around me turned into a blur. It felt like someone knocked my legs out from under me as I collapsed to the hard cement floor. Allie started crying and hugged me as I sat, crumpled on the ground. Both her and her dad were saying something to me, probably telling me how sorry they were or that they were here for me but everything just sounded muffled and far away. It felt like hours that I sat there on the floor in shock. Just seeing his face, hearing his voice, feeling the hug he gave me before we left for the concert, but it must have only been a minute or two. My Uncle Robert helped me stand up and walk to the car. I was glad he was there because my legs felt like wet noodles and I could hardly walk on my own. As we got in the car I saw the area to the side of the stadium with ambulances and cop cars blocking the view, which I was grateful for. Cops kept greedy nosy onlookers back and I felt a pang of rage at them. How could they be so disrespectful? Didn't they know how awful this was? But it was quickly replaced by a cold numbness that took over my whole body. Allie cried hard and held my hand in the back seat of her dads car as he drove us home. I couldn't help but just stare blankly at the floorboards. I didn't feel like I was crying but tears still streamed from my eyes, forming little puddles as they fell on my jeans. When we pulled in and got out of the car, my mom ran out of the house and gave me a big hug while petting my hair. Her tears cooled my cheek and once again I could tell she was talking to me but I couldn't hear much of it as everything was still muffled. This time however there was also a high pitched ringing in my ears that I wished would go away. I surprised myself by mustering up enough strength to talk but it didn't sound like my voice. It was small and strained, like a child that had been screaming too much. "Mom? I'm sorry, but can I just go to my room?" She looked at me with what was supposed to be sympathy but I saw something else in her eyes. Was it disappointment? Anger? Disgust? I couldn't quite tell, but I didn't care. She hesitated but put her hand on my cheek, clenched her teeth for a moment then gave a weak smile. "Ok honey." She walked past me to hug Allie and Robert. Allie called to me as I slowly stepped inside the house. "Are you sure you don't want me to stay with you?" I turned back for a quick second, forcing the tiniest smile. "No, I'm sorry, I just....I just need some time alone for a while. But I'll call you first thing tomorrow. Love you Allie." She smiled weakly and nodded through her tears.

As I trudged upstairs my feet felt like they were made of lead. When I got to my bed I collapsed on it and its like the dam that was holding in all my emotions suddenly burst wide open. I started violently crying, my whole body shaking, I could hardly breathe. I pulled my pillow to my stomach and curled around it, crying out in pure agony. Every ounce of energy I had was draining out of my body at lightning speed. All I could see in my mind was his smile. I felt like my soul was being ripped from my body and everything I had was suddenly gone. Before long, there was no energy left and everything started to fade into black as I fell asleep, still in my clothes. I woke up some time later, confused and disoriented. My light was off and the blanket was pulled over me, my mom must have come in at some point. I couldn't remember my dreams, just a vague sense of panic and loss, like I was missing something. When the memory of what had happened hit, it was like a lightning strike in my heart. I instantly started bawling again as I sat there in the dark. It was just before dawn, which meant I hadn't been asleep for very long, but try as I might, I couldn't go back to sleep. Every time I tried, I saw his face or some happy memory would flash through my brain and I started crying again.

Chapter 16

By the time it was close to 9am I had cried just about all of the tears I possibly could and was numb again. I felt myself starting to fall asleep again. But then I heard the doorbell, waking me from my near slumber. I went downstairs to see who it was, hoping to see Allie. My mom opened the door and there stood the judge and his family. It was customary for the judge to give his condolences when a member of the Guard died, but I was still shocked to see them. The Judge took my mom's hand in his as he offered his deepest apology. His wife wiped a tear from her eye, trying not to disturb the perfect makeup. It was then that I noticed Liam standing behind his mom. From my place at the base of the stairs I could see him perfectly. He held his head down with his hands clasped down in front of him. But when he glanced up I saw the slightest grin on his face. It was probably undetectable to everyone else but I could see it clear as day. He was happy about this. No....he was....proud. My core began to burn with rage as my mind instantly started putting the pieces together. I remembered being in the car after the incident on Judgment Day when my dad said that Liam was so furious that he was telling his dad that he wanted him executed. About how mad he was when he just let my dad off with temporary suspension. My dad heard it all, even from outside the booth. Liam happened to look up and our eyes met for just a brief moment but it was all I needed to have my theory confirmed. He had a wicked grin and a cold, smug look in his eyes. He might not have moved his mouth but I could almost read what he was thinking right on his face. "Yeah you little bitch, it was me that got your good for nothing dad killed. But what the hell are you gonna do about it you little human?" I couldn't stand to look at him anymore. I ran off to my room and he went back to pretending to be sympathetic. I slammed my door, grabbed my pillow and screamed into it as loud as I could, knowing that the wolves would be able to hear it but not giving a shit. As I watched the Judges car and his security detail drive off down the street I texted Allie. "I need to talk to you in person….NOW!" My phone dinged right away. "Of course." After a few minutes the doorbell rang and I made sure to get to it before my mom could. "Its fine, it's just Allie, I really need her right now." I said as I opened the door and pulled her in for a hug. My mom started to say something but decided against it and went back to her room. I pulled Allie upstairs before anyone could say anything else and closed the door. "What's going on? You know I'm here for you." She sat on the bed and gave me a sad, empathetic look, patting the bed next to her for me to sit down. "No, I can't. I….I….." She watched me pace furiously and got up to grab my shoulders, forcing me to stop and look at her. "Christina, what is going on?" I tried to steady my breath and clear my racing thoughts. "I….I know what happened to my dad. It was Liam Bradford." Allie was caught off guard and let go of me. "What? What do you mean? How?" My heart felt like it was punching me over and over from inside my ribcage as I told her everything. "I don't have any proof but I know it was him. Or probably someone he hired so he wouldn't have to get his hands dirty." Allie was having a hard time processing everything so she stayed quiet for a while until she finally snapped out of it. "Okay, well, it does make sense, but you said yourself, you don't have any proof at all. At this point its just a theory, no one is gonna listen to you. Even if you were a Devout, this is the Judge's son, no one would believe you for a second. We have to be smart." "I know. But I have to do something." Allie grabbed my wrists and made me look into her eyes. "Christina, please, please promise me you won't do anything stupid! I can't lose you too!" I searched her big honey brown eyes as they began to glint with tears forming. They were so beautiful and held such sorrow. She was practically screaming with her eyes to stay with her. Her face that was usually so happy and bright, like a ray of warm sunlight on a cold day was now so sad and scared. I had never seen her like this. I just nodded and gave her a hug. "I promise, we'll get that bastard for what he did! We just have to be smart about it. My dad should be able to look into it under the radar & get any kind of evidence there is. They would be way more likely to listen to him than they would be us." I took a long slow breath and it felt like the first time I had really breathed in the last couple of days. "Yeah. I just…I just can't stand him! But once again, you're right."

We tried to change the subject and spent a few hours just hugging and talking about random things. After a while we both felt better and she stretched and stood up. "I need to get back for a while, but if you still need me it can wait." "No, its ok. I know your dad will be wanting you back for dinner. I'm doing better. Thank you for coming." She smiled warmly. "Don't mention it! You know I'm here for you, always. And I'm just right next door or a call away if you need me. I'll talk to my dad about looking into Liam." I stood up and hugged her tight, breathing in deeply her scent of vanilla and amber. It soothed my soul just a little bit and I smiled. "I know. Thank you. I love you Allie." My cheeks felt warm and I shoved the butterflies that were in my stomach down as I had been doing for a couple years now. We headed down stairs and hugged once more before she left out the door. I started to turn back to the stairs but I couldn't help but overhear my mom talking to one of her friends on the phone and stopped to listen for a moment. "I know, I can't believe he's gone. There's so much to take care of. Luckily most of the funeral arrangements are being taken care of by the department, but still. I don't know what I'm gonna do. No, they still don't know who did it. I bet it was a filthy Vermin like that one he let go a while back. I know, I was so mad at him for that. This was his first night back after suspension too. Normally he wouldn't have been on the perimeter. That's a lower position but he had to start at the bottom. Who knows, maybe if he had just went after that little Vermin, none of this would have happened…" I couldn't listen to any more of it. I was grinding my teeth so hard that I thought I might break my jaw. I went upstairs and threw myself onto my bed. "How the fuck can she say that!? She's practically blaming him for his own death! That… that bitch!" Now my tears weren't from sadness but pure anger and frustration. I hardly slept at all the next couple of days. Every time I did, I dreamt of him. It was so nice, but then I'd have to wake up and my heart would get ripped out once again.

CHAPTER 17

I stood in front of the mirror staring at what seemed like a stranger. My hair was pulled out of my face with a black headband, I had on a floor length black dress with sleeves that went to my elbows. Nothing seemed real, like I had slipped into an alternate reality. Walking down stairs, getting in the car, going to the cemetery, it was all a numb blur. My body was moving but my mind was gone, lost in some dark, cold place. Even seeing the casket lowered into the ground wasn't enough to shake me from my detached state. So many people hugged me, offered their condolences, and I'm sure I thanked them but to me they were all blobs of color with muffled voices that I wished so desperately to get away from. I didn't want to be here. The numbness was starting to fade but in its place was a crippling anxiety that made me want to run as fast as I could. My eyes started darting around to find somewhere that I could run off to, when Allie hugged me tight. Its like the world came back into focus and I wrapped my arms around her. The tears that I thought had all dried up started flowing effortlessly again.

She didn't leave my side after that. Even when we went home, she stayed with me. I crawled in my bed and she laid next to me just hugging me. I knew that I would never be able to thank her enough. She soothed my soul more than anyone else. My cheeks grew warm and for a split second I was overtaken by emotion. "Allie....I...I need to tell you something." "Of course. What is it?" Looking into her rich brown eyes, still red from her own tears. I realized how messed up this was. I couldn't say that. Not right now. Instead I just smiled. "Thanks for always being here for me. I don't know what I'd do without you." She smiled and hugged me again. "Of course! You're always here for me too. You're my best friend and I couldn't live without you either." After a while my face felt tight from drying tears, my eyes stung and my head throbbed. I don't remember falling asleep, but when I woke up several hours later, Allie was gone but there was a note on my bed next to me. "Hey girl. I had to get home but I knew you needed your sleep. Please call me if you need me. I'll check up on you soon. Love you. -Allie." I rolled over to stare at the ceiling, but my exhaustion took over once again & I fell back to sleep.

Chapter 18

The next week went about the same. But I had to go back to school sometime. I took a long shaky breath before stepping foot into the high-school. It was like some sort of movie. Everyone started whispering when I came in. I clinched my jaw and just tried to ignore it. At lunch I went to my locker just to find Blair standing in front of it again. This time she was showing off the new mark on her hand to her friends like it was a huge diamond. "I mean, of course I knew I was Devout, but now its official. I'll probably get my invitation to the Winter Gala sometime this week."

I rolled my eyes. "Could you move?" She looked at me, sneered a bit then moved over just enough for me to get to my locker. I got my keys and walked away as soon as I could. Allie was waiting by my truck. "Ugh. Have you seen little miss perfect and her new ink?" Allie laughed. "Yeah I saw. I think everyone did." "I know. She's even bragging about getting invited to the Winter Gala. I'm so done with all of this." "I know. But your birthday is just in a couple weeks. And I'm gonna make sure it's the best birthday ever." I took in a long sigh then looked at her as I put the truck in park. "Thanks Allie, but honestly, I don't want anything for my birthday. I just....I just can't handle anything right now. It's just too hard without him. Besides, it just reminds me that I'll be the next one to be marked." "I'm sure they'll give you some extra time, given the circumstances." "Yeah maybe, but still….huh….I just wish I could forget all of this."

After lunch I sat in class, lost in thought. The TV screen was playing a movie we were supposed to be watching. It was nothing but the same old history that we all knew forwards and backwards. No one can convince me that it wasn't just an opportunity for the teacher to take a break & pretend to have us actually do something. I just sketched some doodles on the paper in front of me instead of watching it. My mind wandered to what Blair said. She probably would get invited to the Winter Gala. It was a huge party that the wolves had every year at the start of winter. It was held at a huge mansion they used for special events and was their way of pandering to the Devout. Pretty much anyone who was marked as Devout would get invited and everyone else was usually so jealous. Glittery opulence, tuxes, big poofy dresses, ridiculous outfits, amazing food, alcohol, most everyone wished they could go. They called it a charity event but in all reality it was just a big show of wealth and power, like everything the wolves did. Let them have their stupid, boring, stuck up party. No thank you. I glanced up at the TV and I saw that creeps face. Liam Bradford. It was showing the Judge's family, making them out to be some sort of royalty, as usual. My pencil snapped in half as my fist clenched. Suddenly I was back at the base of the stairs, seeing his face. I knew that I didn't have proof, but I didn't need any. It was him, I was certain of it. I tried so hard to shove my anger down but it kept bubbling back up. The bell rang and I walked into the hall but someone bumped me hard from behind, making me trip and nearly fall on my face. When I turned around it was Cory James, one of Blair's little flunkies. "Sorry." He said with a sly grin. Blair and Matt were a few feet away laughing. Seriously? Were they really being this juvenile? It took everything in me to just take a deep breath and walk away.

Chapter 19

go down stairs, knowing that my mom, Allie and our friends from track were waiting to wish me a happy birthday.

As I descended the stairs I tried to give myself a pep talk. "Just smile and act like everything is fine. They're hurting too and seeing you happy will make them happy. Its just for a few hours." When my friends saw me they let out a big, cheerful "Happy Birthday!" It was just a few friends but it was still more people than I wanted to be around right now. Still, I smiled and said thank you. My mom just stood there for a second then gave me a quick and awkward hug and said "Happy Birthday." I put on a great act really. Smiles, squeals when I opened one of the presents my friends got me, eating a big piece of the cake that Allie made me, laughing, you'd almost think nothing was wrong. But when everyone else had left and Allie was about to leave she gave me a big hug and whispered in my ear. "I know you're not ok. But I also know you need some alone time, so when you're ready to talk for real, call me." I gave her the first genuine smile I had all night and told her thank you. My mom didn't even attempt to make conversation after everyone left and just started cleaning so I went back up to my room. I plopped down on my bed, my head swirling with thoughts. I pulled out my phone and looked at my calendar. "That's one down, countless birthdays without you to go." I said to myself. And in just a little over three weeks was Allie's birthday. I scrolled to the next month and there on the 21st was an automatic entry that came on everyone's phones, just like with Judgment Day. "Winter Gala." I thought of all the pictures in magazines and videos I had seen from ones in the past. Some looked like princesses out of a real fairy tale, others wore these weird costumes that were meant to be "artistic" but just looked stupid to me. People would pose for a wall of cameras and commentators would gush about the expensive designers they were wearing. It was ridiculous and at the center of it all was the Judge and his family. Once again I couldn't stop the intense anger from burning me like lava in my chest. I started to daydream about dressing up like one of the Neutrals that were their servants, I mean servers, and sneaking into the Gala. Once inside I'd find Liam and slip some untraceable poison into his drink. Then I'd slip out like nothing happened. "Right. Because that would work. What am I some international spy?" I scoffed at myself. Still, it was a nice thought that helped, if only a little, to calm the rage. I then felt a twinge of panic, knowing that the wolves could come to our door to give me my mark any day now.

Day after day went by and no sign of the wolves. Soon it was Allie's birthday and it went about the same way mine did. Me and our friends at her house, presents, cake, fake smiles, all of it. I had written her a letter that I was going to give her that night but I chickened out and shoved it back into my pocket.

CHAPTER 20

A few days later on a Saturday, Allie texted me. "OMG. They're here! Wish me luck." I looked out my window and saw a black car pulled outside of her house. It was a pair of wolves that were there to give her the mark. "I wish I could be there." I texted back, even though I knew it wasn't allowed. "I have an idea" she texted back real quick. My phone buzzed and the screen said there was an incoming video call. I answered and saw her propping up her phone where I could see her whole living room. Her dad came in, not noticing and opened the door, letting in the two wolves. One was a woman with long blonde hair and the other was a man with short brown hair who held a silver box. "Sit down please." Allie gave her dad a quick hug then sat down on the couch. "Aliyah Rae Larson, we have come to bestow upon you your Class Seal. All pertinent information shall be stored within this seal and must be used when identifying information is needed. If you do not consent to this, you shall be labeled as a Vermin by default and escorted from the city. Do you consent?" "I consent." The woman opened the box and pulled out a silver circlet and placed it on Allie's head. It wrapped around the back of her head with two circles resting at each temple. The wolf tapped one of the circles and they both glowed with a blue ring. After a few seconds it dinged and the blue light turned green. The wolf woman removed the circlet and sat it down for a moment while she pulled out another device from the box that the man still held. It was a black box with rounded corners and had a slot that went all the way through the middle. She picked up the circlet, tapped it again and tapped the black box the same way. They both got a green light that flashed for a few seconds, then stopped. "Place your hand inside here until you hear a ding." Allie did as she requested and a moment later the machine started making noise. Allie was visibly uncomfortable and tried not to shift too much. "Please don't move." The machine dinged again and the noise stopped. "You may remove your hand and reveal your mark." I could sense her anxiety through the phone as I sat hunched over watching the whole thing. She slowly removed her hand and when she looked down, she let out a big sigh of relief, as did her dad and brother. The wolf woman put the things back in the box and locked it. Without saying much, the pair left. Allie hugged her dad and her little brother then said she wanted to go call me to tell me. Her dad said she could and walked off along with her brother. She watched them to make sure they left the room. Once she was sure they were gone she ran up to the phone and grabbed it smiling. "Yes! I knew it!" she exclaimed as she flashed the back of her hand. A black circle surrounding a white N in front of a black hand print, the symbol for the Neutral class. I realized just then that I had hardly been breathing the whole time. But I could finally breathe now. I was so relieved. "That's great! I'm so happy for you." Sure, it wasn't the rich, popular Devout class, but we both hated them anyway. It also wasn't the Guard class where you had to risk your life to uphold dark and twisted laws, whether you agreed with them or not. The Neutrals didn't have it super easy but they got to live normal lives and pretty much be left alone by the wolves. That meant I didn't have to worry about my best friend being hurt while protecting those stuck up snobs like my dad was. Or worse, getting hauled away to live like Dani and Marcos. She was ecstatic and smiling her big, incredible smile. I felt a little flutter in my stomach and remembered the letter. "Oh hey, at some point I need to give you something." She barely heard me over her own joyful squeals but said ok.

That Monday she showed off her new mark to all our friends.

Most of whom had already gotten their marks as well. There were a couple Guards but most of our friends were Neutrals. Our friend Hayden looked over to me. "I'm surprised you haven't gotten yours yet." Allie could sense my hesitancy and spoke for me. "With everything she's been through they're giving her a little extra time." "Oh of course! Why didn't I think of that? Well I can't wait till we all have ours." They continued to chat but my mind kept flashing images of that mark on my hand. The creepy looking rat face with scratches across it and lime green eyes that matched the V that it sat between. Those two wolves grabbing me and throwing me down in the sewers, or out in the woods like in my dream. Or maybe they would just kill me right then and there to save themselves the trouble. It was getting harder and harder to pretend that everything was going to be alright. My grades were slipping because I couldn't focus on anything. The only part of my day that made it easier to think was when I was in practice. Running helped clear my mind, but not for long.

CHAPTER 21

Allie stopped me one Friday just before I went to my truck after the last bell. "Hey, you know I'm here if you wanna talk right? I feel like we haven't really talked in a while." "I know. I'm just....I'm not in a great place right now. Half of me is terrified to get marked but the other half just wants to get it over with because I'm so tired of this waiting game." She grabbed my hand. "I know. But its gonna be ok." I pulled my hand back. "No Allie, its not. You and I both know exactly what's gonna happen when I pull my hand out of that machine. They're gonna know how much I hate them and I'll get taken to the sewers or out into the woods to die like an animal." Allie bit her lip and tried to think of something comforting to say quickly, though it was pretty obvious that she knew I was right. "Listen, just try to think about something other than the wolves. If you can stop hating them, or at least stop thinking about how you hate them, until you get marked, maybe that'll help." "That's not how it works. They don't really know exactly how it works, but its something deep inside of someone, maybe even something in their DNA. People have tried to fake it and its never worked." I leaned against my truck and took a deep breath, then grabbed my backpack and rummaged through it for my water bottle. When I did, a folded up piece of paper fell out. I picked it up, remembering what it was. "Oh, hey, I almost forgot. I was gonna give this too you a while back but I was waiting for the right time. Well, seeing as how I could get marked any day now, you should probably go ahead and take it. Just wait till you get home to read it. I gotta go. Love you." After handing her the paper and giving her a quick hug I got in my truck and drove off, gripping the steering wheel. My cheeks were hot and I felt like I could hardly breathe.

Up in my room I paced back and forth waiting for a response. I replayed every word of the letter in my head, halfway regretting having ever written it. "Allie, you've been my best friend for six years, but it feels like its been as long as I can remember. You've been there for me when no one else was. You are absolutely amazing in every way. With everything that's happened, I have a feeling that things are gonna go from bad to worse. I know you don't want to lose me, but I'm afraid you're going to either way. I hate the wolves and everything they stand for. I always have. I know I'll be marked as a Vermin. And if that's the case, I might as well try to do something meaningful. I don't know exactly what that is yet, but I want to help open people's eyes. I want to show them that they can't just treat us like insects. I'm sure there's some good ones out there, but there are so many that are drunk with power and it has to stop. I would love it if you'd help me, but I know that's too much to ask. But before anything else happened, I wanted to tell you something that I've been hiding for a long time. I love you Allie. Not just as a friend. You're so beautiful and I've had these feelings for a while now but I didn't want to freak you out or ruin what we had. I probably wouldn't even be telling you now if it wasn't for everything that's happened. I totally understand if you don't feel the same way, and hopefully we can still be friends. When you get done reading this, text me. I'll probably be too embarrassed to talk, but you can text me." I kept pacing until I thought my carpet would catch on fire. "Ding". I shakily unlocked my phone and clicked the text icon. "Of course we're still friends, nothing could ever change that. And you better not do anything stupid cuz....I feel the same way." I just stood there staring at the last part of her text with a heart emoji. This was the first time in months that I was actually happy. I couldn't stop myself from jumping up and down a little and squealing, making me feel like a 5 year old. But in that moment, it was exactly what I needed. My heart was pounding but this time it was for a happy reason, rather than anger, fear or sadness. "Ding." "So…can I call now?" "Yes." When I heard her voice it was like I was hearing it for the first time. It was so smooth and sweet. "I guess we were both hiding the same thing huh, go figure." She laughed and I felt my body relax, something that I had almost forgotten how to do. "Yeah, I guess so." "I've felt this way for a little while, but with everything you've been through, I figured I'd wait to tell you because you definitely didn't need any more big changes in your life." My cheeks would probably be sore the next day from smiling so big, but I didn't care. I felt like I was about to float away. We talked for hours, and while we did that all the time, this time was different. Finally it was time to hang up, even though I really didn't want to. "I…I love you Allie." "I love you too Christina." I pressed the hang up button and fell back on my bed with the biggest smile on my face.

Chapter 22

I just knew the wolves would be coming by the next day because nothing can ever go good for very long without something horrible happening right after. But the day came and went with no knocks. I talked to Allie all day on the phone through the weekend, anxiously waiting for the inevitable. On Monday when there still hadn't been a peep from the wolves I walked into the school holding Allie's hand. Our friends saw and ran over to us. They were so excited and happy for us. But with every passing minute the anxiety at the back of my mind got louder and louder. Another day with nothing. Then another, and another. I didn't even care that Blair and a lot of the other kids in school were whispering about Allie and I being together. Their weak attempts at taunting did bother me at all, it was so inconsequential compared to the sword that was hanging over my head. I just did my best to pay no attention to them & be happy with Allie. And I was happy. Happier than I even thought was possible.

Friday I was sitting on my bed trying desperately to focus on my homework when my pen dropped and bounced under my bed. When I reached under to get it, my fingers hit the hard edge of a wooden box. I pulled it out and sat with it on my bed. How could I forget that this was here? My hand slightly trembling I opened it to see stacks of old pictures. My dad and I at the father daughter dance when I was 8, my 5th birthday party where he tried to do magic tricks for all of my friends, me as a baby wearing his police officer hat. It was like a bubble had burst. Even with the kids in school being obnoxious, and even with the threat of the wolves showing up, for the most part I had been truly, blissfully happy the last week with Allie, but it all seemed to fade away and I was thrown back into the harsh reality. My dad was gone. No, he wasn't just gone, he was taken from me. By that bastard Liam. I knew he had to be the one that got him killed, but there's no way anyone would listen to me, especially without any proof. Tears of anger and sadness blended together and launched a full on assault on my eyes. I started thinking again about when the wolves came. There was no doubt that I would be marked as a Vermin. The hatred I had for them burned so deep that there was no chance I could hide it. They were going to take me away, away from everything. My life was destroyed when my dad died but I was just starting to pick up a few of the pieces and be happy with Allie, now I was going to lose her too. They would take me off to be sterilized, then shove me in the sewers or worse. I looked at my phone. It was the 20th. It had been a month and a half since my birthday. They would be coming any day. Probably tomorrow or the next day. My mind was so crowded with thoughts, like I had 20 different voices screaming at me at once, all while my heart beat pounded like a big drum in my ears. I knew I couldn't let them take me like that.

So once again I grabbed my backpack, stuffing it with anything and everything I could. I made sure to bring a couple changes of clothes, some water, what little cash I had saved up, my journal, and anything else I thought I may need. I gripped the knife that my dad had given me in my hands. It meant so much more to me now. "I'll always keep you safe." "I hope you do keep me safe dad. I'm sorry, but I have to do this." I put on my baseball cap, opened my window and snuck out just as I had when I went to the sewers, only this time I got in my truck. Before I turned the key over I took a deep breath and texted Allie. "Hey. I've been so incredibly happy the past week. I really do love you and I know that you're probably gonna hate me for this, but I have to go. I can't get marked as a Vermin and end up like Dani's sister, or worse, eaten down in the sewers. I'm gonna try to do something good though. I don't know exactly what, but something that will make some kind of difference. I'm so sorry. Love you." Just before I started my truck I sent a quick text to my mom. "I have to go. I won't be coming back, don't look for me. I love you. I'm sorry." The engine turned over and I turned off my phone and threw it in the passenger seat.

CHAPTER 23

As I drove my heart pounded. What was I doing? I couldn't get help from anyone or I'd put them at risk. You can't get a hotel room without a mark so where could I go? I drove around for hours before finally deciding to pull into a dark area on the outskirts of town. I was getting low on gas and so tired that I could barely keep my eyes open. I just reclined the seat and tried to get some sleep. The anxiety and the cold made it hard and I mostly tossed and turned in the uncomfortable seat all night. When the sun finally came up I went to a gas station, put a little gas in my truck and got a Danish for breakfast with the cash I had put in my backpack. The day crawled along at a snails pace as I sat in my truck, not wanting to waste gas. I knew that my phone could be tracked but I finally had to turn it on for something to do as it turned into late afternoon. I saw I had a couple texts from Allie but I wasn't ready to open them yet. I couldn't stand to have her pleading with me to come back or telling me she loved me, I just couldn't handle that right now. Instead I just scrolled through social media for a few minutes, trying to distract myself. A text popped up from Allie and I was just about to dismiss it, thinking it would be another "I love you" or asking me to come back, but then I read the words on the screen and a chill ran down my whole body. "They're here." When I opened the text I saw a picture that Allie had obviously taken out of her window. Even though it was a little blurry, you could see a black car parked outside of my house with two wolves walking up to the door holding a silver box. My time had officially run out. They'd come looking for me as soon as they found out I was gone. In a panic I shut off my phone and started driving but I had no idea where I was going. After a while I realized that I was completely lost and turned down a winding road with perfectly manicured trees and big nice houses with gated fences. Streetlights glittered and it almost felt like I was in a completely different place. I wanted to turn around but there were a couple of cars behind me and nowhere to turn. The road made another bend and then opened up to a big expansive plot of land with a brick fence and beautiful iron gate. Unlike the others however, these gates were open with guards standing at either side. I pulled off down the side street where there were less streetlights and more modest houses. I parked for a second then turned around to look. The cars that were behind me went up to the gate and, after presenting their hands to the Guards to be scanned, drove through and up the long driveway to a huge mansion. "The Winter Gala!" I said to myself. I had totally forgotten. My brain buzzed with thoughts all at once. "Shit! I have to get out of here, if anyone catches me I'm done for!" But just before I started my truck another thought crashed through my mind. "But wait...Liam is here. What if....no, I'm not in some spy in a movie, I'll never get close to him and even if I did, what would I do? But if I could just see him one last time, make him admit what he did...." My adrenaline was pumping so hard that all rational thought got washed away. I grabbed my knife and got out of the truck, being careful to stay as well hidden as I could. Luckily anyone that would have seen me was too busy letting in rich snobs to notice. I ran across the street to the large brick fence and started to climb. When I jumped down on the other side I winced both in pain and in fear that someone had seen me. However the house was pretty far from the fence and in this part of the courtyard it was relatively dark as the sun was nearly fully set. There weren't as many cameras along this side of the fence so I was able to slip passed at just the right moment when the cameras swept by the other way. I found a decent hiding spot behind a big hedge that seemed to be hidden from the cameras. I waited there, panting and trying to clear my mind enough to form some sort of half-assed plan. I was so paralyzed in thought that I hadn't realized that almost an hour had passed when I suddenly heard a voice. "I don't have long, my mom has me watched like a hawk but I had to get outta there. Its so boring I feel like I'm gonna puke." No. It couldn't be. This was too easy. It was Liam. He was on the phone with someone and had walked off from the house. He was no more than 25 feet away from me. My heart pounded as I tried to think about what to do, what to say. "Yeah its so dumb. We have to go out here to this stupid stuffy place and act like we give a damn about these filthy little humans. I don't care if they are Devout, they're still humans. I don't know why we treat them like their practically equals when they're not. When I'm in charge some things are seriously gonna change." My fear turned to rage and I moved by instinct alone. I pulled out my knife from my pocket, opened it and came out from my hiding place. "Liam!" He turned around to face me but looked utterly disinterested. "I'll call you back, have to deal with some trash." He hung up the phone than sneered at me. "Who the hell are you?" I tightened my fist around the knife and the belt clip dug into my skin. Through gritted teeth I spoke in a voice that I had hoped was powerful and intimidating but just sounded shaky and weak. "Of course you don't remember. I know you were the one who got my dad killed!" He looked me up and down and narrowed his eyes a bit. "Wait, was your dad the one that got my phone smashed on Judgment Day? The one who wouldn't go after that little pest that tried to kill me?" I just stood there, shaking uncontrollably with anger. He started laughing. "Aw, poor little human. Missing your daddy? Well maybe he should have listened to me. I said I wanted him executed. My dad wouldn't do it, but guess what? He's not the only one with power. A call or two later an wouldn't you know it, he ends up dead. I'm just sorry I wasn't there to sink my teeth into him myself. Maybe if he wasn't such a little bitch he'd still be here." I couldn't take it any more. I lunged at him, catching him off guard. He swiped at me, hitting me and sending me to the ground. I coughed and tried to catch my breath while he laughed. "Did you seriously just try to attack me? Wow you really are dumb." He started to come at me but I rolled out of the way as quickly as I could. I got behind him, leaped up and drove the knife blade down hard and fast, without even thinking. It struck him hard in the back and he lost his balance, falling on his face. My eyes shot open wide, realizing what I had done. I went to his side and looked in horror as blood began to pool around him and he made raspy gurgling noises. Tears streamed down my face and every nerve in my body was on fire. I had hit him on his left side, I had…..I had hit him in the heart. I knew if I pulled out the blade he would only die faster but if I left it in, they would be able to find out that it was me. Before I could think about it any more I heard a big commotion and could tell that Guards were headed over to where we were. I looked again at his face as it lost all color. His eyes were wide in shock and he was barely breathing through the blood that spilled from his mouth. The Guards were shouting now, running up with flashlights and tasers drawn. I quickly grabbed the handle of the knife and, with a little effort pulled it from his ribcage, then ran off. With adrenaline coursing through me, it almost seemed like I flew over the fence and hopped down. I didn't bother with my truck, I knew I could get away easier on foot. All my years in track paid off in that moment as I ran faster than I had ever run before. I turned down every side street I came to, trying to not stay in a straight path. Sirens blared all around me and I just knew they'd get to me eventually but I just kept telling myself, "Don't. Stop. Running." I hopped over fences, dashed through backyards and sprinted down dark alleys. After what felt like hours I had to stop to catch my breath. I wedged in-between two dumpsters in an alley and tried to take slow, deep breaths. When I could breathe a little better I listened carefully. The sirens were still wailing but they sounded far away. I stepped out and looked around, trying to take in as much information as quickly as I could. I had no idea where I was, but it seemed like I was at least close to the city limits. It was darker and quieter out here, which was to my advantage. I could keep running out of town and into the woods, but that's where the hunters patrolled and they would probably be out there in grater number now. When I thought of the woods, I saw my dream again and shuddered. No. Not there. I had to stay in the city, but out here where it was darker and less occupied. I could tell that the sirens were coming from my right so I started running in the opposite direction, trying to put as much distance between us as possible. I had no idea how long I had been running, but it had to have been for most the night as the sky was starting to lighten. Before long I was barely jogging, dragged down by pain and exhaustion. I knew I needed to stop. There was a little sliver of space between two cinderblock fences that was open to the alley but closed off from the street view. I slipped in there and got as far in as I could. My legs collapsed and I rested my back against the hard fence, appreciating the tiny bit of warmth it still radiated from the sunlight it had absorbed all day long. Still the December air was cold and stung my burning lungs. I put my knees to my chest and hugged them tight for warmth. The sirens were barely audible now and I could finally start to relax a little, but as the adrenaline started to wear off, I began to realize just how much pain I was truly in. My legs felt like they were seized up cement, my feet ached from the many rocks I ran over, my ankles felt like they would shatter if I jumped over one more fence, and my chest hurt so bad I could hardly take a breath. My hand slipped in my pocket and pulled it out. The knife still covered in drying blood. "What have I done? I....I.........I killed him." Tears burst from my eyes, making my eyes hurt even more than they already did. I felt like a child who was lost in a grown up world. So lost, so panicked, so helpless. All I wanted was to close my eyes and wake up from this nightmare. I'd go downstairs, hug my dad and give him a big kiss on the cheek before calling Allie and telling her about my day. We would talk for hours about BKR and school and I wouldn't need to be running for my life. But no matter how hard I wished, when I opened my eyes I just saw the same dirty, leaf littered hiding place. One of the times when I closed my eyes, I actually fell asleep, overcome by the deepest exhaustion I had ever felt.

CHAPTER 24

Rather than a nice dream, or even a bad one, it was just black until a noise startled me awake. My eyes darted around but I let out a sigh of relief when I saw a squirrel rummaging around in the leaves about 10 feet away from me. I sat up, scaring it off, and took a moment to get my bearings. I didn't have anything with me. My backpack, my truck, my phone, it was all left behind. What was I going to do? How could I possibly survive? I may not have been marked, but I may has well of been because there was no way I could go back now. My heart sank at the thought of never seeing Allie again but this time my eyes couldn't muster up any tears. My eyes were dry and felt like they had gravel in them. I knew I couldn't stay in any one place for long, but I had no idea what to do or where to go. The more my brain tried to think logically, the more fuzzy it got. One thing was certain, I had to avoid any cameras, something that wouldn't be very easy. At least out here it was better. People had cameras at their front doors, but not back here with the dumpsters. However if someone came out to throw out some trash, they'd spot me. I had no idea who to trust so I just had to avoid people at all cost, human or not. As I walked, my mouth felt more and more like a desert and I knew I'd need to find water soon. One of the houses had a low enough fence that I could peek over. It didn't look like anyone was home so I hopped over and went to the side of the house where a faucet stuck out of the wall, attached to a long hose. I turned the valve only a little to not make much noise and pulled the end of the hose to me.

The water flowed down my throat and was the best thing I had ever tasted. I heard something so I quickly turned the valve off and ran back to hop over the fence. As the sky grew more dim I squeezed between two houses. So I could rest. I had to stay low to avoid a window, but thankfully it had thick curtains that were pulled closed. As I leaned against the wall by the window, trying to absorb the bricks warmth,I could hear someone's TV turned up loud. At first I didn't pay any attention until I heard something that made my heart nearly stop. A TV anchor on the news. "The Judge and his family are in mourning as their beloved son was brutally murdered by a human. Surveillance footage has produced this image, however it is our understanding that this person has not yet been marked. So please, if you see this girl or anyone acting suspiciously, especially if they do not have a class seal, please report it to the authorities. Do not engage as she may still be armed and dangerous." "Shit!" I whispered to myself. Why was I so shocked? Of course they had plenty of pictures of me, there were cameras everywhere and not only did I sneak onto the Judge's property, I ran all over town. The gravity of my situation really started to set in and my tears returned to me. Yeah, I may have just turned eighteen, but I was still basically just a kid. And now I was public enemy number one. This was bad. Very, very bad. I knew what I was going to have to do. I started walking again until I came to a street. There it was. When there weren't any cars I lifted the manhole cover and climbed down the slimy dark stairs again, just as I had before. This time however I didn't have a flashlight so I had to walk completely blind.

CHAPTER 25

The smell made me lightheaded but I pushed on. After a couple hours of walking and not seeing anyone, my exhaustion and rumbling stomach became too much to bare so I sat down and leaned against the wall. Down here I felt less exposed and could breathe a little easier, figuratively at least.

A hand shook my shoulder, waking me from my dreamless sleep. When I opened my eyes I saw a woman's face and I jumped a little. "I'm sorry, didn't mean to startle you. Are you ok?" She had messy, tangled dark blonde hair with pink ends and tattered, dirty clothes. She held a flashlight in one hand and I could just barely see the Vermin mark. "Yeah I'm.....well.....no, I'm not. Do you have anything to eat?" she smiled, "Yeah come on, we've got a colony not far. Its not much but we have what we need at least. I'm Tessa." I followed her for a while and when we took a turn I saw the tunnel widen in to a hub where different sewer lines met. There were some tents and some people moving around the camp. "Hey Misha, I found a new one. Can you grab her something to eat?" A guy with dark skin and tight braids nodded and went into one of the tents. "There's 15 of us including you. We're one of the biggest colonies in town." Misha came back with some sandwiches. Or, rather some deli meat between two stale pieces of bread but I still devoured them. Misha laughed. "Girl you really must have been starving." I nodded through big bites. He handed me a bottle of water that I guzzled down. After I was done, Tessa looked me up and down. "So how long have you been down here anyway?" I swallowed the last bit of water. "Not long. I was gonna get marked and I ran away. This was the only place I could think to go." I figured they didn't need to know all the details, especially since I wasn't sure I could trust them yet. Tessa sat next to me on the ground and a woman walked up behind her, resting her hand on her shoulder. "Hey babe. I'm gonna get some rest." Tessa kissed her hand. "Okay baby, I'll be there in just a bit." As the woman walked off I started asking questions. Any filter I normally had was gone and my sleep deprived mind just spilled it all out at once. "How do you guys survive down here? How long have you been here? Why don't you stand up to the wolves?" Tessa looked a little shocked, then laughed. "Wow, you got a lot of questions. Okay, well, I've been here for a while. I was taken down to the sewers 9 years ago but I've only been here in the colony for a about 4. Its hard, real hard. It's a little better out here. The closer you get to the city, the harder it is. We mostly steal stuff when we can, but we scavenge & hunt too. We all try to help out in any way we can. On our own there's no way any of us could stand up to even a single wolf. That's why we stay together. The city workers don't come down here as much this far out and the wolves don't come down here much either." She leaned in and spoke in a softer tone. "Don't go telling everyone, but we're planning on fighting back if we can get enough people with us. The wolves hate it down here and some people think there may be a reason for that. There's rumors that some people have found silver not too far from here, that its in the rock just behind the layers of brick and cement. That's why the wolves don't like it down here." My heart raced. "What!? Silver? But....but I thought...." She reached into her pocket. "I know. We all thought it wasn't possible, but one of my friends gave me this." She pulled out a little lump of shining metal no bigger than my thumb. "But, how can you be sure its real silver?" She got a sad look on her face. "The guy who gave it to me, he was like a big brother to me. Not the strongest, but he was smart. He got into a fight with a wolf that tried to attack him. He touched it to the wolf and he cried out like he was in pain and shifted back into human form like he couldn't control it. Unfortunately that one wasn't the only wolf down here. He got hurt real bad but was able to get away. He gave it to me just before....just before he died." A tear fell from her eye and she wiped it away. "I'm so sorry." She smiled and shook her head a bit. "Thanks, but its fine. It happens a lot down here. It was a few years ago and people have been searching for more ever since. We actually managed to get a little bit, but its slow going. We just don't have the tools we need to bust through the thick walls. They made it nearly impossible. Which I'm sure was their intention. Its gonna take some time, and maybe a miracle , but if we can get enough, we might just be able to start fighting back." My eyes stung with tears, but ones of hope and joy. "That....that's amazing! Someone has to stand up to them. The lies, the death, all of it has to stop. I want to help in any way I can." My excitement at this new found knowledge couldn't stop my eyes from fluttering as they tried so desperately to close. Tessa laughed. "And we'll take all the help we can get, but girl, you're about to pass out. Why don't you get some rest." She waived Misha over and he took my hand, leading me over to an open tent, showing me where I could sleep for the night. It was nothing more than a pile of dirty tattered blankets on an old, thread bare cot but I was grateful for it and laid down. "Thank you." "Don't worry about it girl, we look out for people here." He said as he gave a warm smile and walked out of the small tent. Laying down on the cot, my body ached as all my tense muscles tried to loosen & relax. My eyes slammed shut and I fell into the deepest sleep I had in weeks.

The next morning I woke up to a commotion and went to see what was going on. The people of the colony were gathered around Tessa and another man with long black hair in a stained brown coat. He held a piece of paper in his hand and it was clear that he was upset. "What's going on?" Tessa looked over to me with a serious , somber expression. "Christina, you're awake." The man looked at me and angrily held up the piece of paper with my picture on it. "You! This is you isn't it? The guards came down here and are asking if any of us have seen you. They say you killed the Judge's son! They said if we help you they'll send the wolves down here to track us all down and kill us! You have to get out of here, now!" "Zane, just calm down and let me talk to her, okay?" "Fine. But make it quick." Tessa took a deep breath and walked over to me, pulling me aside. "Listen, I...I wanna help you, I do, but..." Swallowing hard and taking a deep breath, I tried to sound more confident than I felt. "It's okay, I get it. There's no sense in risking everyone's life for me. I'll go. Thank you for helping me." She gave me a sympathetic look, a quick hug, handed me a flashlight. Then she slipped something cold into my hand. "Good luck kid." I glanced down and saw the lump of metal in my palm. I gritted my teeth to stop the tears from forming and gave a little smile. "Thanks." She turned to walk back to the others and I walked down the tunnel that lead us here. No matter how hard I tried to hold them back, when I was out of sight, the tears started falling down. Eventually I came to a ladder and climbed up it.

Chapter 26

I got back up on the street, dusted myself off and started walking but then I heard sirens behind me. I took off running as fast as I could. When I turned down a side street I stopped so fast that I nearly fell on my face. A cop car blocked the road and two Guards stood with their tasers pointed straight at me. "Freeze!" Glancing behind me, I saw another cop car and two more Guards. I felt like an animal that had been backed into a corner. My heart booming inside my chest, I started to turn down the way I had come but a cop car rounded the corner on to the street where I had climbed up from, blocking my only other exit. I thought about trying to run in between some houses, or anywhere I could but apparently the Guards could almost read what I was thinking on my face. "Don't move!" Out of sheer panick I shifted my weight, readying myself to run but just then the Guard pulled the trigger. Two darts soared towards me faster than I could blink. They easily slid through my clothes and dug into skin, sending an intense shockwave of electricity coursing through my body. Every muscle locked up, sending me crashing to the ground. My nerves felt like they were on fire and I was completely paralyzed. Two of the guards came up from behind where I had been standing and put one heavy boot each on my back, pushing down and driving me further into the jagged asphalt and gravel. The lightning strikes ended and my whole body went limp, still sore and tingling. They pulled my wrists behind my back and handcuffed them. It took some effort for them to drag me to my feet and I struggled to stay standing as my muscles had not yet gained their full strength back. As they pushed me towards the cop car, my legs shuffled and stumbled and I struggled to catch my breath. I got shoved into the back seat and they slammed the door, making me jump a little. For a few minutes they stood around congratulating each other, then got back in their vehicles. The officers didn't say a word as they drove. All of this was so surreal. I had skipped class a couple of times, snuck out of the house once, but other then that, I rarely ever got in any trouble. Yet, here I was, in the back of a cop car, the most wanted criminal in town. How the hell did this happen? "This has to be a nightmare." I thought to myself. But it wasn't.

CHAPTER 27

Before long we pulled up to a building with a big statue of a wolf. It was Marrok in wolf form. Standing tall like a man, with the fur and head of a wolf. It was majestic and intimidating, as intended, but it also filled me with a mix of emotions. I understood why he did what he did, but it lead to all this. And now the wolves were no better than the humans were back then, enslaving and killing those they held power over. But I didn't have long to think about it until they parked and yanked me out of the back seat. Their hands gripped my biceps tightly as they walked me through the large metal doors and into a dimly lit room to stand before a plain front desk. They said something into their radios and a minute later a couple of wolves came out with a silver box. Instead of standing there, just holding the box, the male wolf set the box on the desk then came behind me. He gripped my arms as the officer unlocked my cuffs and took them off. I struggled against his grip but there was no use. He squeezed so hard I felt like my bones might break. He held one arm behind my back and put my left arm out. The woman pulled out the machine and placed my hand inside. She tapped it and a green light started to flash. I felt a burning sting on the back of my hand and closed my eyes. After only a few seconds she pulled the machine away to reveal a black circle with a lime green V and a creepy rat face. They didn't even bother to use the scanner, not that it would have mattered anyway. The Guard behind the desk scanned the mark and the wolf forced my arms in front of me so the other female Guard could replace the hand cuffs. She walked me down a hallway with barred cells on either side. Most were empty but a few had people in them that watched with dead eyes as we passed. When we got to the end of the hall there was a big metal door with spots of rust all over it and just one small window with closely spaced bars high up above my eye level. Another Guard stood by the door and placed his hand on a pad that dinged. The locks clicked and the door opened. She unlocked a barred door and slid it back into the wall. Before me was a small cell with nothing but a cot and toilet. Nearly at the level of the high ceiling was the same type of small window, the only source of light. She pushed me forward into the cell then slid the barred door out from the wall and locked it again. "Hands through here." The Guard tapped a small rectangular hole in the bars. I did as she said and she removed the cuffs. She pointed to a light grey jumpsuit that was folded up on the cot. "Put that on and place your clothes through here." I went to the cot and picked up the oversized jumpsuit. "Can…I have some privacy please?" She huffed. "No can do. I have to watch to make sure you don't try to sneak anything. Take off all but your underwear. Now hurry up." Humiliated, I peeled off my clothes that were stained with blood and dirt and quickly stepped into the jumpsuit. It was baggy and the fabric wasn't comfortable, but at least it was clean. I wanted to slip my knife out of my pocket before I handed her my clothes, but I was past any delusion of escaping. She took the folded clothes that I passed through the slot, then shut the big thick metal door, leaving me there in silence, all alone.

A while later, as I sat on the hard cot, once again clutching my knees, I heard the big heavy outer door begin to open. I don't know why I had a twinge of hope but it quickly vanished as a Guard stood before me, giving me a look of utter disgust. He looked familiar with his light blond hair and green eyes. On his uniform was a badge that read "Officer D. James." This was Dillon James, Cory's older brother and one of the few guards that weren't appointed their position, but requested it. He had actually been marked as a Devout so when he asked for the position they knew he'd be perfect for the job as he clearly had no sympathy whatsoever for his fellow human.

"Christina Redding. You have been charged with the murder of Liam Bradford. And before you try to deny it, there's more than enough evidence. You really are a fucking idiot aren't you? I can't wait until next Judgement Day. It'll be the most exciting one in years. Welcome to your new home for the next several months. Personally I say why wait, but living in here, day in and day out will be torture so I guess it's fine. You'll get 3 meals a day and you'll get up to 2 visitors every weekend for one hour, other than that, get comfy because you're stuck here until Judgement Day. May their Judgement be swift and your death be slow and painful." He walked out for a second then came back with my Uncle Robert. I was so happy to see him that I instantly burst into tears. I ran up and gripped the bars, wishing so bad that I could give him a hug as I choked on my words. "Uncle Robert! I....I.......I'm so sorry! I....please, you have to help me!" I looked at him with eyes so filled with tears that he looked blurry. But even through the tears I could see that the soft, loving face I knew was gone and in its stead was one of cold anger. "Are you serious?" I was bewildered and my mind couldn't understand the harsh tone in his voice. "Wha…what do you mean? Uncle Robert, its me." "I'm fully aware Christina." "Please, uncle Robert, I never meant for any of this to happen, its all just so….messed up. I…I…" "You killed a man. And not just any man Christina, you killed the Judge's son! Do you have any idea what that means? Not only did you evade your seal, you killed the judges son!" "He killed my dad! He said so himself, he hired someone to kill my dad, your best friend! I didn't mean for this to happen, I just….I got so mad, and he came at me, it just happened so fast." "You don't think I know that Christina?" Shock and confusion had my brain spiraling. "What? You…you knew that it was Liam that got dad killed?" "Of course I did. Aliyah told me everything. Even she hadn't, I already suspected it. And maybe with enough time, I could have gotten the evidence and presented it to the judge. But you had to take it all in to your own hands and ruin everything."

I tried to process everything but it felt like I couldn't think at all. "But…even if you had, he would've just gotten a slap on the wrist, you know that! He murdered my dad! How can you be saying all this, he was your best friend! I love you Uncle Robert, please, at least tell me you understand." "No Christina, I don't. Yes, he was my best friend and I was devastated when he died but he and I both swore an oath to uphold the law for the greater good. Do you realize that because of what you did, everyone is going to suffer. They're tightening down on everything. We're lucky they haven't decided to go on a killing spree just to prove a point." "But Uncle Robert, that's the point, they're monsters and somebody has to do something! How can we all just go along with it? This is demented! We outnumber them, we can stop this, why can't anyone see that?" He sneered in disgust. "You really are a Vermin aren't you. You're dad would be so disappointed in you. You put not only your own life at risk, but everyone's. Yes, the laws are harsh, but as long as we follow them, things are just fine and the majority of people stay safe and happy. It's horrible that some suffer but we have to think of the greater good. The needs of the many have to take precedent. Allie has been utterly broken since you left, how could you do that to her? I remember when you and Allie met as little girls. You with your little pigtails and Unicorn backpack. But right here, right now, I don't recognize you at all. All I see is a murdering Vermin. Starting tomorrow I'll let Allie come to visit you for now, but I don't know how long I'll allow it. I want her to get over you and move on. I won't be coming back. On Judgment day you will be executed and I will console my daughter. Goodbye Christina." He turned to leave and they closed the big heavy door. I felt like what little pieces of me were holding on had been shattered into dust. His words hurt worse than anything else that had happened to me in the last few days and I collapsed to the floor clutching my chest sobbing uncontrollably. It was like there was a black hole in my heart sucking every bit of my soul into the void. Guilt and fear overcame me and I curled into a ball on the floor. Images kept flashing through my mind. My dad, the knife he gave me with its inscription covered in blood, my Uncle

Robert's face on the other side of the bars, Liam's face as it turned white and blood gurgled out of his gasping mouth. Uncle Robert was right. This was all my fault. Everything went black as I let myself fall asleep crumpled up on the hard floor.

CHAPTER 28

The next morning I got woken up by a creaking door, only to see Dillan James standing there once more. He pushed a metal tray with food through the rectangular hole in the bars and tossed it, causing it to come clattering to the ground. Half of the food went flying but I snatched what I could and shoved it in my mouth. I wasn't even sure what it was, all I could tell was that it was mushy and flavorless but it was food. As I ate, Dillon just stood there, watching with his arms crossed. Even though I tried to ignore it, the anger in me started to rise. "What? Do you really have to stand there and watch me eat? Haven't you humiliated me enough?" His cruel laugh bounced through the concrete and metal hallway. "Oh this is nothing. You have no idea what's coming to you, you filthy little Vermin." "What is your problem? How can you betray your own kind like this? I'm a human being, just like you." He scoffed. "Like you? No. I'm nothing like you. You're a little Vermin and a murderer. I mean come on, how stupid do you have to be to kill a wolf? No one has been dumb enough to kill a wolf in decades and you not only killed a wolf, but the Judges son! But hey, at least this years Judgment Day will be exciting. There haven't been any executions in a while, and I can't wait to see yours." I clenched my jaw, unable to hold back the anger any longer. "Just go! Why are you here?" He got his face close to the bars and looked me straight in the eye. There was so much darkness and vitriol in those eyes. "Because its fun." He laughed and leaned back. "Besides, I'm here to tell you that you get to have some visitors today. After today it'll only be on the weekends. Visiting hours start in a couple hours." With that he turned, shut the door and left me alone again.

A couple of hours later the door opened again. "Come on, hands through here." I placed my hands through the hole in the bars and handcuffs were once again put on my wrists. The bars slid aside and another officer placed shackles around my ankles that had a short chain between them. They connected the handcuffs and shackles with yet another chain, making it impossible to raise my arms above my waist. Latched onto the central chain with a thick, locking buckle was what looked like a chain dog leash with a leather grip.

The guard yanked on the lead chain, forcing me to move forward. I had to shuffle my feet to not trip. He led me to a room with a bench in front of a wall covered by a curtain. He unlatched the central chain once again allowing me to lift my arms. Before I could say a word, he pushed me in and then stepped out of the room and shut the door. I heard a buzz and then the curtains parted to reveal a thick plexiglass wall. On the other side sat my mom and Allie. "Allie!" I ran up to the glass as fast as could I with my short shuffling steps, and put my hands up to it, rattling the handcuffs. She ran up to her side of the glass and put her hands where mine were. "Christina! I've missed you so much!" Tears streamed down her face and I could tell she had been crying for quite some time. "I missed you too. I'm so, so sorry!" she shook her head. "No, don't worry about that now. We don't have very long, I just want to be with you." She put her forehead to the glass and I did the same. For a couple of minutes we stayed that way, sending our spirits through the thick glass, searching for a connection. Then I remembered something. "Allie, I left my journal in my truck, and I'm sure they took everything but I made a digital copy and saved it in my email. I need you to go to it and read it. I'm not expecting you to agree with it, but maybe it'll help you understand how all this happened. Please, please read it. And let others read it too. Maybe, just maybe it can change some minds." "Ok, I will, I promise." I gave her my log in info and she repeated it a few times to ensure she'd remember it. "Christina, I'm so sorry for how my dad acted. I'm furious at him!" I took in a long sigh, remembering the sting of his words. "Its okay. I'm just glad you're here." We talked for a little while, then my mom stood up from where she had been quietly sitting. I had almost forgotten she was even there. "Allie sweetheart, its nearly time to go, let me speak for a moment." "Oh I'm so sorry, of course." I was so hoping that my mom would be distraught, crying, and say how much she loved me, but I could tell by her face that this wasn't how it was going to be. "Christina." I had never seen her face so cold before. It's like she had turned to pure stone. "Mom, I....I know I messed up, I'm so sorry. I never meant for any of this to happen." She thought about her words carefully before speaking. "Sorry? Christina, I already lost my husband, now you've taken my daughter from me too. I love you, but I can't bare to see you this way. My daughter is sweet, smart, talented, and a little rebellious at times, but over all a good kid. You....you are not my daughter. I will pray for you to find peace. Goodbye." Somehow, even though I wasn't surprised by her reaction, I still felt a pang of guilt and panic in my heart. My mom went to the door on her side of the room and pressed a button. A guard opened the door and escorted her out. "Time to go miss." "Please, just 1 minute." Allie ran back to the glass and put her hand up to it. I'll be here every chance I get. And I promise I'll read it. I love you!" The Guard cleared his throat and Allie reluctantly turned and left. After they were gone, the curtains closed and the guard came in and attached the lead chain. I shuffled back to my cell and got the shackles and handcuffs removed. When the big metal door shut, I laid on the cot and let the tears pour out. It seemed like all I had been doing for months was crying. I didn't know what was worse, Uncle Robert and my mom being so disappointed and disgusted with me, Dillon and his taunting, or Allie being so lost without me. It was all just too much to bare.

CHAPTER 29

With nothing to do, no one to talk to and nothing but bland grey all around me, I started to think I would die of boredom before I ever got to Judgment Day. It had only been a few weeks, but it already felt like an eternity. I laid with my back on the floor, staring up at the high cement ceiling when the door opened. Without moving I rolled my eyes, bracing for the clattering of the metal tray on the floor. "Breakfast Vermin." I was getting so use to Dillon and his insults that I didn't even look over to him. "What? No little quips this morning? Nothing to say? Did I finally break your spirit? Damn, I was hoping it would take a little longer. Maybe even a few punches. You're no fun." I just rolled my eyes, trying to not give him the satisfaction of a response. "Go away." He huffed and shut the door. I rolled over to my side so I could sit up and when I did, something caught my eye. The morning sun came in through the small window and was glinting on something under the cot. I reached my hand under and felt a lump of cool metal. Butterflies fluttered in my stomach as I felt a tiny hint of hope for the first time since I had been here. It was the silver that Tessa gave me. It must of fallen out of my pocket when I took off my clothes. I was shocked that neither I nor the Guard noticed but I was extremely grateful. Clutching it to my chest I tried to contain my excitement and calm my racing thoughts. For a while I envisioned doing something big and dramatic. The Guards were human so it wouldn't have any effect on them, but I'm sure I would get close to a wolf on Judgment Day. Maybe I could sharpen it into a spike & hurt one of the wolves with it. "And then what?" I whispered to myself. Even if I could manage to hurt one wolf, there would be others, and Guards, and a whole stadium full of people. I knew I had to do something with it, I just had to give it more thought.

When it was time to see Allie again, I made sure to hide the small lump of silver in my pocket before they took me into the visitor room. I was glad that they didn't care enough to watch or listen to us. They were confident that no one would be stupid enough to try anything, and that hubris was to my advantage. I still spoke low just in case one of them did decide to take their post seriously. "Allie, I have something that could change everything." "What?! What do you mean?" "It's a long story, but I just need you to take it." I pulled out the thin rough oval like blob of metal and held it up just to where she could see it peeking out of my hand. She sat there staring at it with wide eyes. "Is….is that what I think it is?" "Yes. Apparently its down in the sewers just behind all the thick concrete walls. I don't know how much is down there, no one does, but it could be enough to turn things around. I've tried to think of some way to use this, but there's just nothing I can do from in here. If you take it, you can show it to people, give them hope. They'll be more willing to fight against all this if they have hope." It was just thin enough to push through one of the small round holes in the plexiglass. Once it plopped into Allie's hand on the other side, she gripped it and shoved it into her pocket. "I'll keep it safe, I promise." I nodded. "Don't show it to your dad, or anyone until you're absolutely sure you can trust them. I love you." The door started to open and we tried to seem as normal as possible. "I love you too." Allie stood up and left the room, stopping to glance over her shoulder and look at me longingly, just as she did every other time. For the first time, I felt like we may just be able to turn the tide after all.

Chapter 30

The days melted together and I lost all track of time. The only way I knew what time of day it was, was by the mushy, unappetizing food being dropped into my cell. On the Weekends Allie would visit me, telling me about more that she had read of my journal. I could tell that she was starting to truly understand, and if anything good came from all this, it would be that. Months went by and with every passing day the mountain of fear and guilt began to collapse, leaving a massive crater. I was finally starting to accept my fate as my optimism all but vanished. And it definitely didn't help that Dillon was constantly counting down to my execution.

"I get what you mean Christina. Something has to change." This would be one of the last times I got to see Allie. "I'm so glad you agree. Have you been getting it out to people?" She nodded. "Yes. Its kind of hard to know who to give it too but I have hundreds of copies printed out and I've been giving them to people I trust. We have a couple dozen people who are on our side now. Its not much, but it's a start." I smiled weakly. "That's good. At least my death will mean something." Allie put her hand up to the glass. "You're not going to die, okay! I'll….I'll think of something. I refuse to let them do that to you! I still have the…..the you know what. And I have someone who's been going down there to look for more. We've only got a little bit so far, but it's a start. I'll talk to someone, make something out of it, I'll, I'll…..I don't know, but I'll think of something! " "Thank you Allie, but its ok. There's nothing you could do for me. You already tried convincing your dad to say something to the Judge, you even tried talking to the Judge yourself. He doesn't care if his son got my dad killed, he was still his son and he's not going to let this go. If you try anything else, you'll just end up here too and I can't have that. I need you to get more people willing to stand up to the wolves. Maybe, with enough people and enough… you know what… they can actually take down the corrupt, power hungry wolves." I whispered to her through the plexiglas. Tears welled up in her eyes. "I'll… I'll do something I promise!" I just smiled and put my forehead to the glass, knowing that there was little to no hope. I knew she would beg and plead with her dad no matter what I said, but I also knew that he didn't want to help. To him, I was already dead. But I had come to realize that my life didn't matter, what mattered was what could come of it. For now, I'd just try to stay strong for Allie, she was all that I truly cared about.

Chapter 31

"Wake up Vermin. The big day has finally come!" I opened my eyes slowly, steadying my breath. Surprisingly, at this moment I wasn't very scared, just numb. As always, he put on the cuffs, shackles and lead chain. I shuffled down the long hall, passing all the empty cells.

Looks like they had saved me for last.

The clattering of the shackles chains echoed through the halls eerily. We turned down another way that I hadn't seen yet. Two Guards opened some large heavy doors and I was suddenly blinded by bright, summer sunlight. After spending months in a quiet, dark cell all by myself, the bright light and roar of the crowd felt like an assault on my senses. The Guards stopped for a moment and I wasn't sure why. Once my eyes adjusted and everything came into focus I saw the Judge's podium far in front of me with two wolves standing on either side.....in wolf form. I had never seen a wolf like this in real life. They would be beautiful if they weren't so utterly terrifying. They stood tall with broad shoulders and their faces were those of growling wolves. It was then that my heart began to pound.

Dillon yanked on the lead chain, pulling me to the side where he lead me to a big cage with a several other people inside. Some of them I recognized as some of the people from the Colony, though I couldn't remember their names. I got shoved in after the lead chain was removed. The announcer started the same old speech I had heard a million times. That this was a sacred day of justice that kept our world safe, how we owe our existence to Marrok and the Great Uprising, and all of that. I turned to the others in the cage. Some were crying, others were shaking in fear, some just looked defeated. I had seen them in the other cells but didn't know most of them. In our dusty and dirty grey jumpsuits, we really did look like caged animals, stripped of all color and humanity. One after another, the Guards would pull one out and lead them to a stand right in front of the Judge's podium. A lawyer would read out what they were accused of, be it theft of food, getting in a fight, or not cooperating with authorities.

Those were the ones from the colony and I knew it was my fault. They wouldn't give me up and got taken in. But what had happened to Tessa and Misha? Did they get away? What about Dani and Marcos? Since they weren't here, I had to assume they were safe. At least that's what I wanted to believe.

Most of the prisoners got taken to the left where they were strapped to a steel table and had a tracker implanted. It wasn't great, but at least they got released after that. The ones from the colony weren't as lucky. I couldn't watch so I closed my eyes and tried to ignore the cheering crowd as they were taken to the execution platform. Luckily they were given first degree so it was quick and painless. I could here the device go off and the crowd going nuts, but at least they didn't have to scream.

Then I heard a familiar voice. "Time to go." I opened my eyes, hardly able to believe it. "U…Uncle Robert?" "Come here." I wanted to hope but his voice was steady with no emotion. I came close and he attached the lead chain. He lead me to the podium but all I could do was look at him, searching for some glimmer of recognition, empathy, something. When I got to the stand, he pulled back the little door and ushered me in. The podium was wooden but reinforced with a metal frame. I looked ahead of me to see the Judges stand. It was a desk like podium in ornate carved wood that towered above me. On either side two wolves stood in wolf form with crossed arms just staring at me, snarling and growling. The Judge looked down at me, his eyes burning a hole right through me. A lawyer came up to my right, "Christina Redding you are accused…" but before he could finish, another wolf came up from behind me, speaking in a smooth, beautiful, but powerful voice. "There's no need. You are dismissed, Mr. Jackson." The wolf came around to stand in front of me. A beautiful woman in wolf form. Her fur was more auburn than the other two that were more grey. Her eyes pierced mine as she spoke again. "Christina Redding, you have been charged with the murder of Liam Bradford……my son." My mouth ran dry. This was Amelia Bradford, Liam's mom and the Judges wife. "Judge Bradford, what punishment do you see fit for this Vermin?" The Judge rose from his chair and placed his hands on the desk in front of him, his head hung low. The whole stadium fell eerily silent. When he spoke his voice echoed through the thousands and thousands of seats. "I decree that this Vermin, for the charge of killing Liam Bradford, my beloved son, shall be executed….to the third degree." The audience was deafening as they cheered, shouted, and whistled. It felt as though the Earth was going to open up beneath my feet. Everything grew muffled just as it had when my dad had died. How….how could this be really happening? My Uncle Robert attached the lead chain and pulled me back out of the podium and pushed me to the right, leading me to the platform. A shining, polished marble platform with 2 tall steel posts with chains hanging from them. As I shuffled towards the platform I kept telling myself, "No, no, something is gonna happen. Uncle Robert will do something. Say something Uncle Robert, please, say something!" But he stayed silent. I got to the platform and the two wolves that had been standing on the side of the Judges podium came up on either side of me. They grabbed the thick metal cuffs that were attached to chains on the posts and clamped them on to my wrists, locking them. Only then did they remove the ones I had already been wearing, but they left the ones around my ankles. One pushed a button and the chains retracted, pulling my arms out to the side until I screamed in pain. I heard a pop and knew that my shoulders were dislocated. What's worse, I heard the audience laugh when I screamed.

I saw my uncle Robert standing just off the platform, his hands behind him. He refused to look at me but I tried to call out to him.

"Uncle Robert, please, please help me! Don't let them do this!" He stayed as still as a statue. I heard something behind me then I saw the Judge come around to face me. He stood there and put out his hand, his robe fluttering dramatically in the hot breeze like some sort of villain.

A wolf came up with a long box. He opened it and pulled a long, shimmering sword from it and handed it to the Judge.

CHAPTER 32

The Judge admired it for a moment then stepped up on the platform where he stood just a foot or so away from me. "Please, I...I didn't mean for any of this to happen." He took a long deep breath. "Goodbye miss Redding." He moved so fast I didn't even know what happened at first. What was this cold feeling in my gut? Why was everyone cheering so loudly? Its like everything was suspended in time and I had forgotten everything. But then I looked down. The sword was driven through my abdomen, nearly to the hilt. It didn't even hurt. I felt it slide through me as he pulled the sword out. It's silver blade was red with dripping blood. He had a satisfied grin on his face as blood began to gush from my wound. The pain began to creep in, until it was unbearable. I screamed and it only egged the crowd on. Through tears and weakening screams I looked to my Uncle Robert. His eyes were closed, his jaw clenched tight and tears streamed down his face. Then as my body began to feel weak and cold, a heavy hand rested on my left shoulder. A claw scratched my neck as it pulled my hair to the side. Hot breath spoke in my ear. It was Mrs. Bradford. "This is for my son." My shoulder erupted in pain as she bit down, her fangs ripping through flesh and muscles. She quickly pulled her head back, tearing a massive chunk out of my shoulder.

Though the cheering crowd was growing more muffled and

distant sounding, I thought I heard something else. Was that Allie? She was screaming. "Noooo!" One last tear fell from my eye but I smiled the weakest smile, knowing that she loved me. Then the world went black.

Its interesting the knowledge you gain after you die. How you can see everything that happened like a movie. I wish I could tell everyone what its like, but I can't. All the pain, the anger, the sadness, was all gone. I was finally at peace. Even though no one else will ever know what those last moments were like, at least I would always carry her love with me.

CHAPTER 33

Allie:

I couldn't' stand to watch, yet I couldn't look away. I gripped the small chunk of silver that I still held in my pocket. When the sword ran through her I lost all of my breath. Which is why I was surprised I was able to scream when the wolf tore into her shoulder. Reflexively I screamed and fell to my knees. "Noooooo!" Mrs. Redding helped me stand up and hugged me. I didn't want to hug her because of everything she had said to Christina, but right then I couldn't refuse. My body shook as I cried uncontrollably. How could this have happened? I just knew that my dad would say something or do something to stop it. Just like they do in the movies. The main character comes close to death but something always happens to stop it. Someone always saves them. How could this be over? "Let's go." Mrs. Redding said in my ear. I hesitated for a brief moment, not wanting to leave her. But then I saw the wolves beginning to tear apart her lifeless body and my stomach twisted so violently that I thought I was going to throw up. I had to leave. "I'm sorry Christina." I whispered under my breath as I closed my eyes and turned away.

Mrs. Redding helped me push through the crowd so we could leave before everyone else. I was starting to feel a burning rage I had never known as I watched the people around me cheer and clap like their favorite sports team had just won the championship.

We navigated our way through the chairs and pushed past the people, my little brother following close behind. We got to the main entrance and a Guard started to stop us but then recognized us. "Oh, Mrs. Redding, its you." He spoke into his radio for a moment, waited for the reply, then nodded. "You can go." Mrs. Redding nodded a quick "Thank You" and walked me to her car. I sat in the passenger seat, tears still flowing but silent. Jake didn't say a word either. "I'll take you two home and wait with you guys until your dad gets home. He'll have to stay there for a little while longer." How could she be so calm? Not a single tear. Maybe it was just shock. But my mind was somehow empty and racing at the same time. She was right. Christina was right. All of this was so gruesome, so dark and twisted, yet we were all so conditioned to it, it was like nothing to most people. I understand why the wolves fought against the humans back then, but this, this wasn't the solution either. They had become no better than the humans they hated. How can a society thrive if one side is a slave to the other? All that oppression just leads to revolution. Then the winners take it too far and the whole damn cycle repeats. Something has to change.

When we got back to my house, I went straight to my room and sat on my hot pink fuzzy comforter. I pulled out the stack of papers I had been hiding under my bed. Her journal. Then I went to my closet, standing on my toes to reach the shoebox from the very top shelf. I opened it, revealing the dozen or so chunks of silver, adding the one that was in my pocket to the pile. Filled with a new and burning resolve, I closed my stinging, tear filled eyes and took a steadying breath. "She's right. Something needs to change. And if she's not the one who will be able to change things, I will."

To be continued.